RETURN OF VICTORY

RETURN OF VICTORY

RECLAIMING HONOR™ BOOK 8

JUSTIN SLOAN

MICHAEL ANDERLE

DISRUPTIVE IMAGINATION

LMBPN Publishing
PMB 196, 2540 South Maryland Pkwy
Las Vegas, NV 89109

First US edition, October, 2017
Version 1.04, October, 2018

RETURN OF VICTORY TEAM

JIT Beta Readers

Kelly ODonnell
Peter Manis
Joshua Ahles
Kimberly Boyer
Paul Westman
Micky Cocker

If we missed anyone, please let us know!

Editor

Lynne Stiegler

Thank you to the following Special Consultants

**Jeff Morris - US Army - Asst Professor Cyber-Warfare,
Nuclear Munitions (Active)
W.W.D.E**

CHAPTER ONE

Over the Atlantic

Valerie had never realized that being alone with her thoughts would be so cathartic, but sailing across the Atlantic by herself certainly provided that opportunity. After her comm device went on the fritz halfway across, she was left staring out at the darkness to the west. She just wished the airship would hurry the hell up so she could get to New York before war broke out.

A part of her still believed there would be a way to mitigate this fire that her friends had started, but the rest of her thought that a final war to end it all wouldn't be the worst thing in the world. Pull out all the rats and cut off their heads, so that they and the disease they had brought upon the lands would be gone once and for all.

That wasn't all she thought about, though, as she sailed. She thought about how she had almost returned to the military compound where she was raised, how she could have very easily touched down in Old Paris and visited her old haunts, searching out clues to her life before she was turned into a vampire. Now that those thoughts were in the past, she realized what a trap such actions would have been. Could she ever have escaped?

Even if she had physically departed, she was certain she wouldn't have left mentally.

It was time to accept that she was a new person, that she had moved on.

Michael's Justice Enforcer wouldn't meander about in her old life. She'd be on the front edge making a difference. For now, that meant defending New York for what she hoped was the final time. After that? She had no idea.

Two thoughts occurred to her, though, as she sailed back. The first was the question of how she would explain the whole situation with faking her own death in New York, if she had to do so. She supposed simply telling the truth would work. The second was about Robin and having left her up north in Toronto. She wasn't regretting that, but she wondered about her, about how they had become romantically involved to begin with. Here she was, this super-powerful vampire, taking a younger, less-experience vampire under her wing, and they had become somewhat involved. Nothing too serious, though it had been glorious. She would never forget the way the woman had kissed her after taking down Slaver's Peak, but they hadn't even gone as far as her and Jackson, and even that wasn't much. Still, had it been wrong of her?

She tried to put herself in Robin's shoes, and wanted to hit herself. A powerful older vampire comes along and gives you oogly-eyes? It would be pretty damned hard to resist. Imagine if Michael, after helping her take down Donovan, had swept her up in his arms and pressed his lips against hers. There was no way she would've been able to refuse. In fact, she thought about it now, imagining the strength, how it would've felt, his tongue— NO! She laid back in the one-woman airship, closing her eyes and sighing.

Promise Number One to herself was never have thoughts like that again. He was with Bethany Anne, in a sense. Two vampires that, as far as Valerie knew, could read minds. Best to figure out how to picture Michael as her grandfather or something, so she didn't get her head ripped off by a jealous lover. *Ah, shit, best not to think of Bethany Anne as a jealous lover, either*, Valerie thought. Another way to likely get her head torn off.

For a moment she pondered the idea of the infamous Bethany Anne, wondering if she really was the type to tear heads off or if Valerie was letting the old rumors of her vampire days with the Forsaken get the best of her.

Promise Number Two time. She swore to herself right then and there to not let romance stuff get in the way of her duty, and to not let herself get in a position where her power might influence someone to go for her.

Promise Number Three. She was going to kick so much ass here that no motherfuckers would ever consider attacking her, her people, or anyplace in this hemisphere ever again. The sound of her feet hitting asses would reverberate across the world, she decided, so that even those back in Europe, Asia, and everywhere else would think twice.

It seemed like she had been sailing for an eternity. But as a gust of wind rocked the ship, she thought she saw something in the distance. Land! She jumped up and whooped, unable to contain her excitement.

"Did you miss me?" she asked as the 'something' grew larger and she could make out the tall buildings and city lights of New York.

She was back, and ready for action.

The comm device buzzed at Sandra's side and she leaped up, reaching for it, annoyed that Diego wasn't there to grab it for her. They had agreed, however, that it was best to take turns at HQ, being ready and making plans for this war that was supposedly going to happen.

All they had so far was the threat Diego had returned with. An army of nomads, wackos, Forsaken and Weres was out there and had teamed up to declare war on New York. While Sandra and the other members of the New York Council were taking every possible precaution—including recalling Valerie and even reaching out to Colonel Walton—they didn't really know how large a force they were up against.

"Valerie?" Sandra asked, having seen the name on the device but still too excited to really believe it.

"It's me, yeah."

"What the hell? I've been trying to get through to you."

"No need, I'm here."

Sandra held the comm device out and stared at it, then pulled it back and said, "Wait...here? You made it? Like, 'in New York' here?"

"As in 'I flew straight back from Europe and am landing in New York as we speak,' yes. That 'here.'" Valerie laughed, which reminded Sandra how much she had missed that laugh. "Where do you need me?"

Sandra thought about this a moment, then said, "Meet me at HQ. We have to brief you on the situation."

"Sure, but first—I don't suppose you've seen Cammie and Royland?"

With a sigh, Sandra replied, "That's part of the situation. I'll tell you when you get there."

"Sandra..."

"Yes, okay? She made it, but she's not here now. She went out to...gather intel."

"Gather intel?" Valerie asked.

"In a sense."

"Sandra, so help me—"

"Okay, okay." Sandra hadn't wanted to tell Valerie and get her worked up, not until they were all in a room discussing it rationally. *Too late.* "The short version is, there's a community out there, one of our new allies, and we think they'll be hit first by the attack. Cammie and Royland had meant to go back to the island, but when they heard what was potentially happening, they volunteered to take a small force and go to the front lines, in a sense."

"Oh my God, Sandra, and you let them?"

"Hey, I've tried talking Cammie out of things before. She's as pig-headed as you are."

"I'm going after them."

"See?" Sandra chuckled despite herself. "Pig-headed. At least come by HQ first, get briefed. Then we can make decisions."

"The decision's made," Valerie replied. "But sure, I want to see you first anyway. I'll be there in ten. But if I am ten minutes too late to help them…"

"I can't wait to see you too," Sandra said and hung up, then rolled out of bed, hoping this stupid nausea would go away soon.

CHAPTER TWO

El Diablo

Cammie glanced around the desert landscape and the town known as El Diablo. It was pressed up against a small hill with dead trees at the top that resembled devil horns, which looked especially ominous silhouetted against the night.

The first thing she had done was come to New York looking for Valerie. When she learned that Sandra had been in touch with her and that Valerie was heading for New York, her first instinct had been to stay there and wait. But the more she heard about the situation, the upcoming predicament, the more she realized that they had to get ahead of this war situation.

So here she was, with Sergeant Garcia and Royland. They had told the others that anyone who wanted to return to the island up north could take off that day. The rest would stay in New York to help fight.

Nobody had left.

It still amazed her that she had gone from the Badlands to this, and what a journey it had been. Now she had Royland at her side, and a group of close friends at her back. While she had felt like quite the badass before, now she stood tall, looking around this land as if nothing could touch her. Like she was on top of the world.

A crunch of rocks on hard dirt sounded behind her and she looked around to see Garcia stepping up next to her. His broad shoulders gave him an imposing silhouette, but he was just one more of her new friends, one more fighter who was with her to kick ass and not bother with the names. Garcia was the only one of the small group to travel out here today who had been here with Diego.

"That's Micky," Garcia pointed out the large man in a leather jacket walking toward them.

"And he's on our side?" Royland asked to be sure.

"This place smells like the devil's butt crack," Cammie noted, scrunching her nose as a gust of wind carried sand and more of that smell. "They should've called the city that instead. El Diablo's Butt Crack."

Garcia shook his head at Royland for chuckling. "Don't laugh at her jokes just 'cause she's your girl, first of all. Second, don't say that kind of shit in front of them, and third...that's not how you say butt crack in Spanish."

She turned to him, waiting, but he didn't offer the translation.

"Good to see you again, big guy," Garcia said, turning to welcome Micky.

The large man nodded, then climbed up to the ledge where they stood. "What, too chicken-shit to just walk into town and see if you get shot or not?"

"Damn." Garcia laughed. "After our welcome last time, I thought maybe you'd want to try to fight Cammie here before deciding if you trust her."

Micky scoffed, but looked at her from the corner of his eye.

"Try me," she said, smiling and revealing teeth that grew sharp as he watched.

"Diego got a sex change?" Mickey looked her up and down, ignoring the growl that came from Royland.

Cammie laughed. "I like this big dude, Garcia. Where'd you find him?"

"Tried to crack my skull open, that's where." Garcia replied.

"And we've been best friends ever since," Micky added. "Well, ever since you soundly kicked my butt, right?"

"Trust me," Garcia leaned in, conspiratorially, "if *I* could take you, you wouldn't stand a chance against either of these two. So we can skip that whole challenge part, right?"

The man had a hungry look in his eyes, but nodded. "I'll take your word for it. Where *is* Diego, though?"

"His woman wouldn't let him come back out to play," Garcia answered with a sneer.

"Sounds like a smart woman. He still wearing my vest?"

Garcia chuckled and nodded.

"No troubles yet?" Cammie asked.

Micky shook his head. "A couple of skirmishes—scouts, I think. And…we might be being watched. But those shit-lickers show their ugly mugs around here, we're ready."

"So, there's no chance of you all simply coming back with us to New York?" Royland asked, although they had been over this in the airship on the way over more than once.

They had brought the airship so that they could ferry people if needed, versus a Pod that would only fit a few of them. The way they figured it, at some point the people might change their minds, especially if the fighting got really bad.

"Wish I could say there was," Micky replied. "These people are loyal to their homes. Many don't even think we have anything to worry about. Way they see it, we've survived out here this long, we'll survive a little longer."

"Damn hubris," Royland muttered, but said no more after a glance from Cammie.

"Well, mister," she nodded toward the town, "I suppose we'd better see this place that's so very precious."

Micky laughed. "I'm sure it will live up to your expectations. Come on."

He led the way past some huts to another large man who introduced himself as Arturo. A redhead poked her head out of a doorway and blew a kiss to Micky, then waved to Garcia before ducking back in. Cammie saw as the door closed that she'd only been in a towel.

"At least you still take baths out here," Cammie noted.

"Ha. Only in our enemy's blood." Micky winked, and Arturo laughed.

They turned a corner as Micky explained to his buddy who Cammie and Royland were, and then a man came charging up and plowed into Arturo. Fists started flying and more of the townsfolk emerged, some rubbing their eyes. They had already gone to bed, apparently, but everyone wanted to see what the commotion was.

Cammie sprang to an offensive stance and was about to charge in, thinking this might be part of the attack, when Micky put a hand on her shoulder.

"Relax, Arturo just slept with the other's girl. Happens quite often out here, or the other way around. Shit, at this point, all of El Diablo has—"

"We get the picture," Garcia interrupted.

"Hey, now," Cammie scolded him. "Let the man tell us about all the incest going on here. I'm curious."

"I never said anything about no incest," Micky replied, frowning. "Ain't none of that happening around here."

"Well, good. Maybe you all can stop fucking and fighting each other long enough to help us kill those assholes out there?"

Micky considered this, then shrugged. "I'll see what I can do." He strode forward and clocked the attacker so hard that the guy fell over unconscious, and stepped up to Arturo.

"It's done!" Micky shouted, finger pointed at his chest. "Got that?"

"He…" Arturo glared, hands still balled into fists.

Micky stared him down until Arturo backed off, and then Micky turned to address the crowd. "Our new friends have a point. For the next few days, or until this's over, we need to pull together, be ready to fight. This isn't about any of us separately, but all of us together!"

A couple of them nodded and others grumbled, but none seemed too eager.

He shook his head, jaw jutting out, then turned back to Cammie and motioned for her and her team to follow.

They went through a low-hanging door into an old house that had been converted into a bar. It still had a couch and a fireplace, but the back half of the room was tables and chairs.

He ordered a bottle and poured glasses of something that smelled homemade, then passed them around.

"These folk, they'll fight the outsiders who've threatened us if it comes to it." He took a swig, not even flinching. "But not many of them have their heart in it. Not after the last little skirmish. We lost a few that day, and…it just took it out of them."

"Maybe if you talk with Pops?" Garcia recommended.

"Pops?" Cammie asked.

"He's the reason most of these people are here," Micky explained, nodding. "We've done enough talking to know he ain't budging."

"Fine. We don't just sit here, waiting. We bring the fight to them, cut off their head, this—"

"Lady Woo," Garcia stated.

"Yes, Lady Woo. From what I hear she's the main problem child, right?"

Micky scrunched up his face, considering it. "Thing is, it might've started with her, but you've got an avalanche now. You don't stop an avalanche by pissing in the snow."

Cammie glared. "First of all, I'm not suggesting we piss on her. I'm suggesting we take her fucking head and throw it at the next in command so hard it kills him or her too. Second, I'm pretty damn sure you *don't* stop an avalanche. You survive it, if you're lucky, but you don't stop it."

He nodded. "That's what we're going for here."

"Then you're a bunch of cowards," Royland said, his voice almost a purr despite the words coming from his mouth. "If that's the case, I don't know why we're here."

Micky moved as if to stand, but at Garcia's head-shake he sat back down.

"How many of us do we need?" he asked.

"To take out Lady Woo? Like an assassination attempt?" Cammie glanced around, her eyes landing on Garcia.

"Oh, now you want my opinion?"

"You're the military man."

Garcia grunted, then looked from their immediate group to the others who had meandered in and found tables to drink at. "With this group, I'd say tactical is better. In and out. Small group."

"So you're thinking…"

"Four. Us four." Garcia smiled as the rest of them frowned.

"Actually, that makes sense," Cammie agreed. "These people want to survive here, they'll need as many as they can to defend the place. And if we want to move fast, worrying about less people and supplies is a bonus. Where do we need to go?"

Micky glanced around the table as if looking for something, then his eyes landed on the cups they were drinking from. He took his and placed it at the edge of the table.

"We're here," he stated, indicating the cup. Cammie's, he placed half-way across the table. "That's the compound Garcia here and his buddies fought at last time, but it's not where we would find Lady Woo right now, I'd think. If she's declaring war, she's probably moved to here." This time he took Garcia's cup, prying it from the man's fingers so that a tad of alcohol sloshed onto the table, and put it closer to Royland. "And you, sir, are New York."

Arturo stumbled up, apparently having just finished a round or five with the guy who had attacked him since they had their arms around each other and their cheeks were quickly turning red.

"If he's New York, we're all fucked," Arturo said with a chuckle.

"Then we best make the…er…best of it!" the other man said, turning back to the bar and wandered away. "Two more, on the double!"

"I'll just absorb the insults in this town and redirect the pain upon our enemies," Royland stated, eyes narrowed but otherwise appearing passive.

"In that case—"

"Don't test me." Royland's eyes flashed briefly red, and Arturo backed up. He pointed to the cup representing Lady Woo's possible location.

"Hey, you want her, not me."

"It wouldn't be so hard to kill both." Royland gave Micky a hopeful glance.

"Please don't," Micky countered, "though I imagine you could simply tear through us all and we wouldn't stand a chance. This man is, believe it or not, my friend."

"Oh, very well." Royland directed his attention back to the table. "How far? From where we are to that cup?"

"A couple of hours, tops. And that's walking. If we take the airship part of the way…"

Cammie shook her head. "I want these people to have an escape route if they need it. Shit hits the fan, it isn't too hard to fly."

"Don't tell Arturo that," Micky replied with a laugh. "Not when he's had this much to drink."

They turned to see Arturo accept the shot from his buddy, and the two threw back again.

"Her," Micky stated, pointing at the redhead as she entered. "Sherry."

"Like the old drink?" Royland asked.

The rest looked at him with confusion, so he waved it off. "No matter. Let's get to it then, shall we? I won't be much use during the day, so if we want to do this without the airship, I suggest we get her trained up tomorrow and rest, then go find this Lady Woo."

"What about the fancy daylight gear you brought from New York?" Garcia asked. "You could wear that and we'd be able to leave immediately."

"I could...but one rip in the fabric, as tough as it is, would not be good for me. If it's all the same, I'd rather fight under the faithful watch of my dear friend the moon."

"And he's right," Cammie interjected. "We need to show Sherry how to operate the ship, and we need to ensure the town's as ready as we can get it in a short amount of time."

"Right." Garcia assessed the glasses before him. "Then we strike there firs—"

"Runners!" A shout came from above, followed by a teenage girl leaping down the stairs, her black hair in a mess and her eyes frantic. "We spotted at least three runners headed this way."

"Three?" Micky frowned, staring at the bottle of alcohol in front of him as if that would help the statement make sense. "What the hell are three runners going to do?"

His eyes went wide with realization at the same time as Cammie said it.

"Bombs! Get everyone down and shoot those sons of bitches!"

Men and women ran past, snatching up the few guns they had and moving to the windows to take aim. Cammie, Royland, and Garcia were right there with them, but Cammie had an idea.

"Can you get to them?" she asked Royland.

He glanced out, nodded once, and was gone in a flash. She knew how he could move, having gone up against him in a friendly match of very violent sparring in the first days after they'd met. If anyone could stop them in their tracks and get out of there before any sort of bombs went off, it was him.

Still, she couldn't let him have all the fun.

"Get shooters on the buildings farther back!" she told Garcia.

"I know!" he shot back, already moving for the door and motioning for Micky to follow.

Cammie ran out into the streets, eyes quickly taking in the night. The moon was a day or two from being full, not that it actually mattered to werewolves. It just helped her understand what the lookouts had seen.

While it wasn't *too* dark, they still wouldn't likely have been able to see more than a couple hundred yards. Based on that, she scanned the desert at the edge of town and spotted one of the would-be attackers.

Another appeared, but a moment later Royland was there, delivering a kick that sent the man flying backward a good hundred yards. The blur that was Royland in the night moved for the next, even as the first one's bomb detonated. Cammie didn't wait to watch it, though, because she'd seen enough to know that Royland had made it, and that although the explosion wasn't humongous, it was more than they wanted in this town.

She reached the edge of town and transformed, her senses heightening and the wind carrying the scent of a woman approaching. Her target. Cammie darted into the night, growling, and saw the woman with a bundle clutched to her chest. It could've been a baby the way she was holding it, but Cammie knew better. Her nose never lied.

With a pounce she was on the lady, transforming back as she landed, grabbed the parcel, spun, and threw it with all her might. It hit the ground a way off and exploded, sending a wave of dust their way.

"Ahhh!" the woman screamed, leaping up as if to attack, but a shot rang out and she fell over dead.

Judging by the hole in her head, it had been Garcia's shot.

She turned to wave in case he could see her, then heard another shot, followed by a ping against a rock nearby. It had come from the other direction.

Ducking low, she transformed again and sniffed the air. Without a doubt there were more out there, but she wasn't sure how many. A dozen, maybe, but it didn't make sense. Why send such a small group?

Not waiting to question it further, she ran out into the night, careful to zigzag across the open area as more shots rang out, pelting the ground nearby.

"Shit!" someone shouted, jumping up from what she now saw was a line of them. They had taken prone positions to fire upon them.

That one went running while two others took aim, but the rest were frozen in fear. *BAM! BAM!* With a ripping pain one of the bullets tore through her back. She imagined it had taken a line of flesh and fur with it as the bullet traveled over her. It hurt, but she had always laughed at how little Valerie liked pain. For Cammie, it was almost part of the fun. A bit of pain acted like three cups of coffee. Now that she had the caffeine effect coursing through her blood, she would teach all of them the meaning of pain.

Hey, why should all the fun be hers alone, right?

She reached them before they could get another shot in. Her teeth tore into the face of the closest, then she moved for the next. This one at least tried to fight, using his gun like a bat on her skull. It nearly connected but whizzed by, and she decided to give him some extra pain for that. First she tore out his calf, then transformed back to her human self as he fell to his knees so she could beat him mercilessly.

Royland ran over and took out a couple more, including the

one who had run. A moment later he was on Cammie, pulling her back from the now-dead man.

"It's over!" he shouted, first holding her back and then wrapping her in his arms. "Calm down."

She hadn't realized until just then how pissed she was. It was like one minute she was having a good time killing her enemies, and the next she was in a rage of blood lust.

In a moment of clarity, she was able to look at herself and see what was happening.

"I thought it might all be over," she told him, pulling back but squeezing his hand firmly. "The killing. The violence."

"You've never been one to shy away from it."

"This is different, though. On the island, I felt something change. I felt belonging. A home. The dream."

He smiled and kissed her hand. "That's the reality. We're just here temporarily to help put a stop to a new evil. That's all."

"And the next evil? And the one after that?"

Royland nodded, looking out at the night. "It's our choice. We can stay on the island, or do our part for humanity. Either way I'll be at your side, loving you the exact same amount."

He stared at her and she thought he was going to kiss her, until he grimaced and said, "Is it weird that the blood all over you kinda makes you *more* appealing?"

"Ugh. God, yes!"

He laughed. "Then, just…one moment." He turned and found one of the men on the ground who was still moving, trying to slither away, and knelt, teeth to neck, finishing him off by taking the blood he needed.

Maybe someday he too could be touched by Michael, as Valerie had been? It didn't matter, though, since Cammie knew she would love him the same no matter what, blood dripping down his chin and in his teeth and all.

Hell, she wasn't much better off after tearing into these bastards as a wolf.

She laughed, and he tilted his head with a bemused smile.

"Aren't we the perfect couple?" she said, gesturing around at the dead and then pulling him in for a bloody kiss.

"We aren't normal," he admitted. "But then again, who *is* normal these days? These guys who try to bomb the town and kill it? That big guy, Micky, maybe? Normal is a stretch."

"Sandra?"

He considered this, then nodded. "I mean, she's having a half-Were kid. Kissed a vampire woman she was a servant to, helped conquer the leaders of Old Manhattan and turn the city into what it is today." He laughed. "If she's normal, so are we. And don't say Jackson with his factions fighting for their turf in the city thing, or Clara and the former pirates. *Nobody* is normal, got it?"

"Blood suckers and shifters are the new norm then?" She considered that idea, then kissed him again. "I like it."

"Come on," he said, putting an arm around her shoulders and leading her back to town. "We've got to get them ready, and who knows if more attackers will show up tonight."

She pulled back from him, biting her lip. "You know, maybe we should stand lookout down here for a few."

"We haven't had much time to ourselves lately," he noted, catching on quickly.

She smiled, wiping a line of blood away from his mouth with her sleeve, then pressing her lips firmly against his as he lowered her to the ground. If anyone else attacked from this direction, at least the two could cause a distraction.

CHAPTER THREE

New York

Valerie took her first step into HQ in what felt like years, but really it hadn't been more than a couple of months or so. How odd it felt, knowing that this building had once been home to her enemies. She had led a siege against Commander Strake and his Enforcers, then hunted him and the CEOs behind him down. The building had become her home after that, but now felt like such a strange, foreign place.

This sensation confirmed something she had been thinking about for a while now—that she didn't belong here. But where did she belong? In space?

With a glance at the skies, she wondered what sort of battles were going on in space right now. Was it possible something could go wrong and it would all be over without her even getting a chance to fight?

Considering the fact that it was Bethany Anne up there fighting for their survival, she was hopeful.

Several men and women in black uniforms passed by, eyes wide at the sight of her. They all knew her, apparently, though she didn't know them. She wondered if they had thought she was dead, or if that ruse had even stuck. Knowing the way information moved around this city, she wouldn't be surprised if it hadn't.

The elevator dinged and there was Sandra, her belly certainly leaving no doubt that the woman was moving along in her pregnancy. Otherwise, she looked the exact same.

Her eyes met Valerie's and the two women ran forward, wrapping their arms around each other and laughing.

"How can such a short amount of time feel like an eternity?" Sandra asked.

"That's a bit melodramatic," Valerie replied, winking to show she was joking. "I see we're not under attack yet?"

"Straight to business, huh?"

"Tell me we can afford not to be and I'll gladly head over to your café for a bottle of wine. No? I didn't think so."

"Diego, Davies, and the rest are upstairs." Sandra led the way back to the elevator and, once Valerie was in, she pressed the button."

"The rest being all but Cammie and Royland?"

"And Sergeant Garcia. He was there the last time, so he went to show them the way. Cammie and Royland aren't really part of the council anymore. Not at this point, anyway. It's like they've moved on."

"I know the feeling," Valerie replied, staring at the wall as she lost herself in the events in Norway. She still regretted the loss of the sweet airship with her symbol carved into its side, but life was full of loss. Better a ship than a loved one.

"Er, right." Sandra glanced at her, seemingly nervous.

"I haven't changed so much," Valerie commented. "You don't have to look at me like I'm a stranger."

"You haven't...and you have."

"What's that supposed to mean?"

Sandra shrugged. "It's like, I see a different look in your eyes, you know? Like you're ready to say good bye to us all."

Valerie bit her lip. That was somewhat accurate, after all. "Not until I know you're all safe. Not until I've taught these assholes a lesson and sent a message so loud the whole world will hear it."

Sandra blinked as if she was holding back something she really wanted to say, but then just nodded. After a few minutes, she said, "I'll be sad when that day comes."

The elevator dinged, and she walked out before Valerie had a chance to respond. Upon opening the doors to the colonel's office, Valerie was pleased to see Diego in there.

He smiled, but the first thing he said was, "I'm coming with you."

"No!" Sandra stepped into the room, shoving him. "Don't you start that, not again. I'm not watching you run out to your possible death while you leave me here again!"

"Can we start with a 'Hey, Val, how's it going' maybe?" Valerie asked, glancing around to see Davies sitting at the table. The office was otherwise unoccupied.

Davies gave her a nod. "Hey Val, how's it going?"

She smiled. "Thank you, that wasn't so hard. Peachy, Davies. A couple of my friends went off into the lion's den without me, and now Sandra here is stalling."

"I wanted to have Diego draw you a map, show you how to get to El Diablo, but instead he apparently wants to act like an ass."

"Our ability to tell her where to go might get her lost, putting Cammie and the others in danger if Valerie arrives too late."

"He has a point," Davies agreed. "It's not like you can just wander out there and find what you're looking for just because you really want to. This is the real wor—"

"Enough out of you," Sandra snapped. "Val, talk some sense into them! You can find the place; you're great with direction. You found your way back from Norway, after all."

"France, actually."

Sandra frowned. "Oh. You…you went back?"

Valerie nodded slowly. "I didn't get out of the airship. I thought I'd want to, but when I was there, I just...didn't feel the need. It's in the past, not a part of me I need to explore anymore."

"All about the next step now, huh?"

Valerie nodded. "That's right. And right now, as much as I want to side with you, Diego has a point."

"Take Davies!" Sandra countered. "He was there."

"He can't heal," Diego argued. "And if you need to move quick, he's not a Were. I'm the right choice, and we all know it."

Sandra looked desperately at Davies, but he shook his head.

"Call me a coward," he stated, "that's fine. But me going back out there? Not very likely unless I'm ordered to, and then it better be alongside a damn army."

"Valerie's better than an army!"

"True, but... Am I being ordered?" He looked at each of them, though none of them were in his chain of command. "If not, I'll have to side with Diego on this. He really is the only option."

"Dammit." Sandra pulled out a chair and sat, arms crossed. She took a deep breath. "Okay, that's decided. I'm over it. Plan?"

Valerie hesitated, but then cleared her throat. "Can we bring everyone back here to New York and then take a strike team out to deal with the enemy?"

"That's one strategy we've been mulling over," Davies replied. "Problem is, some of the people don't want to leave their homes."

"Then we make them."

Diego chuckled. "Yes, that's an option. A very Valerie option, which is why you're in the 'kicking ass' business instead of the 'making friends' business. There's an old man in El Diablo—Pops. He won't go easily, and the folk who live there aren't keen on forcing him."

"There might be other villages too, and other situations like Pops'," Sandra offered. "We can't go around the world making everyone pile into New York. The city would burst."

"So what do you recommend?" Valerie asked.

"We simply have to destroy our enemies," Sandra answered. "Set up in these different towns if we must. Defend and destroy, that's our motto. D and D."

"D and D... I like that. Or the Double Ds." Valerie pursed her lips in thought. "Okay, so if it's all about the Double Ds from now on, why are we sitting around here pulling an SOOA all day?"

"SOOA?"

"'Sitting on our assessment.' Let's get moving."

Diego nodded, gave Sandra a kiss, and said, "Let's go."

"For the record, Val," Sandra commented, "acronyms don't work for everything. Let's leave that to me. Also, don't you let Diego get hurt or you'll be answering to me."

"All about the threats these days," Valerie replied with a laugh. "'Don't let my man get hurt, don't miss the baby.' I get it."

"I'm damn serious about both of those."

Valerie nodded, then held her friend by the shoulders. "I know you are, and I promise to do my best on both accounts."

Then she gave her friend a quick kiss on the forehead. Sandra wiped it off with a confused look, but laughed. "Whatever, just go kick their asses."

"Deal."

"Who said I need looking after?" Diego muttered as he started to follow Valerie toward the hanger bay where they kept the Pods.

He paused to give Sandra a more thorough farewell and convince her he would come back in one piece, leaving Valerie to linger in the hall. She spent the time assessing the places where they had tried to cover up and repaint the holes where bullets had hit the walls. *In a sense, this building was as much a member of the team as any of them*, she thought.

When they were ready, they made their way to the Pods and soon flew out, watching New York grow small beneath them as they rose, then disappear in the rear display.

"She will come after you, you know," Valerie stated. "If you die, I mean. She'll go into the afterlife and pull you right back here so she can unleash her own version of hell on you."

Diego chuckled, glancing back at the city. "I don't doubt it."

"Then we'll just have to make sure you don't take any shit, right?"

"Hey, any plan that involves me not getting hurt sounds good to me." He thought about it, then added, "Or rather, not getting hurt beyond the point of healing. We have to defeat these sons of bitches, and I mean to do my part. Just…if you see any grenades about to take off my head, give me a shout. Deal?"

"Deal."

He leaned forward to assess the ground behind them, and pointed out the direction to steer. Soon they were well on their way.

CHAPTER FOUR

El Diablo

Cammie and Royland meandered back to El Diablo, having spent the evening in each other's arms while she drifted in and out of sleep and he stayed vigilant. The sun was already starting to touch the edges of the dark clouds above, so Royland pushed them to move faster. It wasn't easy waking without much rest, even if Cammie's Were abilities had quickly healed the crick in her neck. The benefits of being a member of the UnknownWorld were immeasurable.

"We might not have much time for that over the next few days," Royland said as they reached the incline at the edge of the town.

"Not weeks? Months?"

"First, I would never last that long. We'd find some dark corner, even in the middle of war. Second, Valerie's on her way back, right? There's no way this war will wear on. I'd like to think of it as more of a skirmish, a bunch of bees found in the school playground that Valerie's going to swat down."

Cammie nodded, licking her lips at memories of his flesh pressed against hers. *Damn, she was glad she'd found this man.*

Judging by the smile he was now giving her, he knew how lucky he was in this situation too.

The smile faded as his eyes moved past hers, and he mouthed, "Oh, fuck."

She spun to see Micky and several of the others carrying a body. They all had blood on them, and cuts.

"Where the hell were you?!" Arturo shouted, storming toward them.

"Arturo!" Micky shouted. They placed the body next to two others. "Not now!"

"No, fuck that! These shit-licking bags of bones just up and vanish on us and you give them a pass?"

Royland's teeth were bared now, but still he kept his cool. He actually had to hold Cammie back, because she was about to slap the shit out of this leather jacket-wearing asshole. Nobody was allowed to speak to her like that.

"What happened?" Royland asked, walking up to Micky. With a glance around, he added, "And where's the sergeant?"

"He went after them to the east," Micky replied, eyes staring blindly in shock. "Three men and two women came in with knives in the night. Nomads, by the glimpses we caught of 'em. Crazy type you don't mess with, but fuck that. Not anymore..."

"They got Pops," Arturo said, his anger crumbling to sorrow. "A knife in the heart, then the bitch slit his throat."

"They ain't holding back," Micky declared, "then neither are we! Get your gear, ladies and gents, we're going to war!"

All those gathered burst into a roar, thumped their chests, and spread out to prepare themselves.

Cammie and Royland shared a nervous look. Damn, so much for the idea of crawling into dark corners to kiss during the war. Based on this, they'd be too nervous to so much as hold hands if it caused them to look away from their enemy for a second.

She sighed with the realization of what this meant. Of how much blood would have to be shed.

"Fuck it," she told Royland. "Looks like the old Cammie is coming out."

"Channel your inner B.A.," he said with a shrug, his eyes smiling despite the worry and anger on his face.

It was almost enough to make her smile, that he remembered how much she used to obsess about the legend of Bethany Anne, or B.A. for short. While she liked the idea of settling down on the island and getting a dog, maybe trying to have a child someday and seeing if that could be a reality, right now it made a lot more sense to channel her inner B.A. and kick some ass.

"Point us in the direction Garcia went," she said, grabbing Micky by the shoulder.

"I don't need to," he replied with a laugh. "Where the hell do you think the rest of us are going? There's no more Pops holding this lot back."

"And this strike against Lady Woo?"

"It'll have to wait." His eyes showed there would be no arguing that. Since she wanted him and Garcia on the mission and felt the people who had attacked during the night needed to pay for what they'd done, she nodded, then turned to see the sunlight now touching the rooftops. "Honey," she addressed Royland, "you're going to have to put on your sun-suit."

"Don't call it that."

She smiled. "Fine. You wear it, and I agree not to call it a sun-suit. What should I call it?"

"Just shut up and kill baddies, and I'll do the same. When this is behind us, you can call it whatever you want."

"Deal." She still wore the smile as she poked him in the chest only semi-playfully. "But you tell me to shut up any way other than jokingly, I'll be pulling off your mask in broad daylight."

"Don't joke like that." He glanced at the incoming rays of light and started for the room where they had stored the protective gear he would wear, compliments of an assassin clan Valerie had taken out near Chicago.

"When he gets back, we're heading out," Micky stated. Then he turned to the others nearby and shouted orders for them to get supplies—whatever they might need, since they weren't sure how long this would last.

Within the hour they were on the move, Royland's grunting muffled by the mask that somewhat resembled an old-style ninja's. It covered his face completely, eyes and all, giving him some visibility but focusing primarily on protection. It was times like these that Cammie appreciated being a Were instead of a vampire.

A few of them walked but the others took the airship for a distance, just far enough to see where the attackers went but not close enough that anyone else should see them. They figured this would also work in that if those on the airship saw something from their vantage point, they could swoop down and alert those on the ground.

"What more can you tell us about this group we're after?" Cammie asked Micky as he checked the tracks left by Garcia.

"Always on the move," he replied, grumbling as he worked on holding his emotions in check. "Good thing Garcia went after them and left this trail, or we might be wandering around out here blind."

"And good thing Garcia's a damn fine soldier," Royland replied, pointing out a shape ahead. As they got closer it was clear it was a body, and not Garcia's. "He might even kill them all before we get there."

They reached the body and Arturo bent over it, then turned to Micky and held up the severed head. "Cut off with his own knife, looks like." He pulled the knife out of the ground where it was stuck beside the head. The corpse was dressed in brown and gray, mostly rags and clothes tied around its neck, waist, and arms.

"He better leave some for us," Micky grunted. "This is them, though. Basically sand ninjas." He glanced at Royland with that

27

last bit, which earned him a grunt of disapproval from the vampire. "Nomads, always on the move, but...this particular group works like mercenaries. They go with the highest bidder, if they don't kill the bidder. Kinda crazy in that way. You walk into their camp, they might just kill you for the fun of it, or you might leave having just bought some of the deadliest killers around."

"Vamps? Weres?" Royland asked.

Micky shook his head. "I should amend that by saying some of the deadliest *human* killers around."

"For the record, we're human too," Cammie corrected him. "Just special."

"That what your momma told you?" Arturo asked.

Cammie glared at him. "You talk about my mom again, maybe I eat your face like I did the bastards who tried to bomb us last night. Put you out of your misery."

"Whoa!" Micky gave her a surprised look. "Getting a little irritable?"

She noticed she was sweating in the heat, and realized that, yeah, maybe she *was* getting a bit pissy. "Just...give me some water and a snack."

Micky glanced around and held up a hand, fingers spread in a signal for everyone to take five.

"Thing about nomads," Royland mused, "is how do you find them to hire them?"

"Ah, and that is the secret," Micky replied. "Makes them much harder to hire, doesn't it?"

"So they're in league with this Lady Woo?" Cammie asked.

"More than likely, paid off by some other group. Maybe the group that attacked last night, probably on their way to connect with Lady Woo. That'd be my guess, anyway."

"Couldn't we then, in theory, just pay them more?"

"Nah. As crazy as those sons of bitches are, they're loyal. Might even be on Lady Woo's side for all we know, having been hired by her many times in the past. Way I understand it, she was using them to take out her rivals out here. Anyone who wouldn't join the network, she made a move on. Once you lose two or three leaders, you start to think maybe you should join up."

"And yet she never took you all out," Cammie noted. "Why was that?"

"Pops was a mean old son of a bitch, but...there was a reason for that, and it's the same reason Pops never let us make a move on her."

"Oh, damn. Don't tell me," Royland said.

"A history?" Cammie asked.

Micky nodded. "Had a kid together, lost the kid...lost each other. How it goes sometimes, but not a good situation by any means. Still, we respected that. Until now, anyway."

"That's why you didn't want to bring the town in on our little assassination plan," Cammie said, realization hitting her like a brick wall.

Arturo was there now, sitting down to join them, and he nodded. "Anyone else had known, they might've told Pops. Would've broken the old man's heart."

"Now we're already on the move." Micky shrugged. "Might still stick with the plan, or see how this goes. Might find us an ally on the way and have a force large enough to attack with."

"You're telling me you know some other groups out here that might be on our side?" Royland asked. "Why wasn't this mentioned before?"

Micky shook his head. "Won't be as easy as that, but if we could convince one or two people we're the winning side, yeah, there might be a chance."

"You're basically saying that if we defeat this merc group, others will take notice and want to be on the winning side?"

"Basically."

Cammie'd had her share of forming alliances and wrapping groups into theirs up north, so she got this and how it worked. "Let's show those sons of bitches we mean business then."

29

With that she stood, took another swig of water, and was ready to move on.

Garcia hid behind an abandoned water tower, one that had fallen over and gone dry many years ago. He had caught up with the attackers just before sunrise, at least the ones who had made the last moves and now took up the rear. Those were now dead, left along the trail as bread crumbs for his companions to find if they deemed to follow him out here.

Where the hell they had gone, he had no clue. But knowing them to the brief extent that he did, he had an idea. Those fuckers were canoodling while he was getting vengeance. And that's how he saw it too. Sure, justice like Valerie and hers were always spouting off about was good and all, but he liked to shove men's fists back into their damn throats when they tried to punch him. Come into a town he was protecting and kill its leader? Oh, you could be damned sure he was going to march right into their town or wherever the hell they lived and deal out some unholy damage.

Right after he got the lay of the land, and paused in hopes of his friends finding him. So here he was, watching and waiting.

The attackers were now taking a break to eat and yell at each other, demanding that some go back to look for the stragglers. He hoped they did, because if Cammie and Royland were back there, he wanted them to get their hands bloody in this mess too. He wasn't greedy. Why should he have all the fun?

He couldn't stand the look of them. Filthy, unorganized—they might be some of the best fighters around, as Micky had claimed before pointing Garcia in the right direction, but they lacked discipline. One was shoving the other, another yelling at him to calm down, but nobody was really in charge here.

If he had just wanted to take them out, now would've likely

been a good time. But that wasn't big enough. He wanted to go to the next level. Find out where the rest of them were, and then take care of them.

He was just about turn and take a well-deserved piss when two of them he hadn't noticed joined the crew from the other side, bringing with them a small boy and his father.

"Get your filthy meat-hooks off me!" the dad shouted. "And if you touch my boy—"

"Shut him up already," one of the men said, and the woman to his right walked up and backhanded the dad.

The boy yelped and shouted, trying to take a swing at one of the attackers while they laughed and shoved him back and forth, and then into the dirt.

Garcia was pissed; this wasn't supposed to happen. His plan was to follow them to their hideout. If he intervened now, he might not find out where it was.

Then again, he realized as one of the men stepped over the dad, shouting something about humility and pulling down his pants as if to piss on the man, he could make them run.

Of course they would flee to the only place they felt safe. He just had to survive the ordeal and be so badass that the survivor, or maybe survivors if he was being generous, would run.

And he sure as hell wasn't going to let Tiny there piss on the dad, not with the son watching. No. Way. In. Hell.

If it all felt apart, worst case scenario was to leave one alive to torture. That would do it.

His drew his knife, aimed at the little target, and let loose. It hit dead-center in the attacker's exposed crotch. As the man screamed and collapsed in a pool of blood, Garcia got up, darted over to new cover behind a car on its side, and unslung his rifle, taking aim through a hole in the rusted metal.

Two of the attackers ran to the spot where he'd just been, but Garcia ignored them for now. His focus was on the woman, who had pulled the knife free and was charging the father with it.

BAM! Her neck blew open, red painting the ground, and the man scampered backward toward his son. Once he had the boy in his arms, he looked around wildly. Garcia spun and took out the other two, who had just spotted him, and shouted, "*Run!*"

The dad just glanced around, confused.

"Run, you stupid son of a bitch, *run!*" Garcia was up now, leaning the weight of his rifle against the car so he could aim and take out another attacker.

They were getting smart now. Out of the remaining three, two dove for cover. One, however, went for the father and the boy.

Ok, maybe not so smart.

Garcia took a couple shots, then stepped out and shouted. The attacker threw himself backward so he didn't get hit, then rolled toward him as he pulled his knives out. He threw one, which would have taken Garcia in the gut had he not moved aside, then ducked back behind cover.

He wasn't out of harm's way here either, though. It turned out that both of the other attackers had managed to sneak around while he was distracted. One came from around the car and the other from on top, both with knives glinting as they thrust and slashed.

Maybe, just maybe, I overestimated my abilities, he thought as he did his best to fight them off. His rifle acted as his shield; he used it to parry the blows as best he could. It was clear they were more skilled than him. Faster.

But he was a military man and, before that, he been a brawler.

He knew he couldn't survive this for long, so he did what he needed to do. While shooting off rounds randomly, he threw himself at the closest attacker's legs with a roar.

To his surprise, it worked. The attacker was caught off-guard, maybe from shock at all the noise. Garcia plowed through him, knocking the man back and into the car hard enough that the car started to rock.

A quick struggle and several slams of the man's head later, and he saw the car start to tip.

Oh, damn.

He rolled out of the way and saw the other attacker leap to safety, and both cleared the car as it landed with a sickening crunch. The two stared at each other for a moment, and then the man lunged. He kicked Garcia's rifle away and came at him, moving on all fours like a dog. Garcia tried to scamper backward but bashed his head into the car, having forgotten it was there.

He saw the fierce eyes, the glint of steel, and the flash of a black boot as it stomped the man's head into the ground. It did that again and again, until finally the attacker couldn't get back up.

Garcia's eyes followed the boot up the leg, and then looked up to see the father there, his son behind him grabbing Garcia's rifle and turning to shoot the others. It wasn't clear if he was finishing them off or just making sure, but what *was* clear was that the boy knew how to hold a rifle properly, and how to operate one too, apparently.

"Who the hell are you?" the father asked, kneeling to take the man's knife and put it to his throat.

"Not yet," Garcia shouted, then repeated himself in a calmer voice. "Not yet. I need one of them alive to show me where their camp or hideout or whatever is."

The dad considered him, then slit the man's throat anyway. There was enough of a twitch to show that the man had still been alive, but then it was done.

"Well, thanks for that, asshole," Garcia grumbled.

"You always talk like that to men who just saved your life?"

"Men?" He glanced at the son. Whatever. "Point is, I saved your lives. And then, yeah, then I suppose you saved mine too."

The man simply grunted.

"What's it to you?" the boy asked, turning the rifle to point it

33

at Garcia. "I would say give me a reason not to shoot you right now, but, thing is, I'm kinda enjoying shooting people today."

"These people attacked us," Garcia replied, starting to rise but pausing when the boy shook his head. "They killed one of ours, a nice old man named Pops."

That immediately got their attention, and the boy lowered the rifle with a silent curse.

"Say that again?" the man demanded. "What exactly happened to Pops?"

"These fighters, these men and women, attacked in the night."

"And Pops is dead?"

"That's right." Garcia couldn't help but notice how their expressions went from angry to sad. "His people are following close, as it is. War's breaking out."

"Sure is," the dad said. "Some tyrants in New York think they can stomp all over us. Well, *hell no* to that, but..." He stopped, turning to his son.

"That's right," the son said, stepping up next to his dad, rifle still at the ready. "El Diablo and its people declared against Lady Woo."

"It sounds like we have ourselves a genuine New Yorker here."

He simply glared, pissed that he had put his mission on the line for anyone that would turn on him like this. It was possible he could take them, but not easily with the rifle aimed in at him like that. So instead he decided to try another tactic, one he didn't like to use too often. Talking.

"Actually, I'm not with New York. Or not originally, anyway. You heard of Terry-Henry Walton?"

The son scoffed, but the dad's face went white.

"Put the rifle down, boy," the man said.

"What?" The boy stepped forward as if he hadn't heard properly. "This man ain't the Colonel, even I can tell that."

"I'm not the Colonel," Garcia said, now slowly standing since he had gotten their attention. "But I am one of his soldiers. He appointed me to New York, to help train their army."

"Bullshit," the boy said.

"I said to lower that damned rifle, boy!" the man said, then turned and snatched it away from the son before holding it out to Garcia. "We'll show you where it is."

"What?" both Garcia and the boy said at once.

"Take the rifle. We ain't your enemy, not if you're with the Colonel." This time he thrust the rifle into Garcia's hands. "Go on. But you better know what you're getting into."

Garcia took it, eyeing the man skeptically. "Why were they... treating you like that? Aren't you on the same side."

"Those sons of bitches ain't on no one's side," the boy answered for his dad. "We were just messengers for—"

"For Lady Woo," the man finished for his son. "But that was before we knew about you. Knew that Colonel Walton was backing a side."

Garcia nodded, looking at them and considering what he'd said. "Here's the deal. We know the people in New York are good people. Lady Woo? She attacked me and my friends before, and we know she's not good people. Why're you with her?"

"It's about survival. We live out in the Badlands. We deal with scum every day. Best way to survive? Form alliances with the good and the bad alike."

Garcia nodded, getting that. He hadn't had the easiest time of it himself before finding the Colonel. "What'd you say your name was?"

"Fred Jones, related to the great Eddie Jones. Ever hear of him?"

Garcia nodded, thinking that rang a bell. "Yes...but I can't place where."

"Out of Queens, before we left. In his day, he did some good. There was one man my family always talked about, one man they respected, and that was because that man saved my Eddie Jones' life."

"Let me guess—Colonel Walton?"

Fred nodded. "The one and only Colonel Terry-Henry Walton. You're with his people, then I'm with you."

The son seemed to be finally grasping what was happening, because his eyes suddenly went wide. "Oh, shit. You mean the same colonel, TH?"

Garcia chuckled. "Try calling him that to his face, see how he takes it. He only lets the very closest to him use his initials. By the book, you see."

"I'd expect nothing less," Fred said, then hit his son in the arm with a gentle *thwack*. "That's Colonel Walton to you. Only," he turned back to Garcia, frowning, "you talk as if he's still around. You've gotta mean his great-grandson or something. Same name?"

"They call me Eddie Jr.," the boy offered.

"And it's a good name," Fred replied. "But shut up and let the man speak."

"You...didn't know?" Garcia asked, unsure if the Colonel would want this out there or not. He'd never really asked or thought about it, but this guy was likely as loyal as they came. "The Colonel, he's not like you or me. He's enhanced."

"Like cybernetics and shit?" Eddie Jr. asked. "Cool!"

"No," Garcia replied with a chuckle. "Like with vampire blood."

He expected them to be surprised, to reject what he had just said, but Fred just nodded as if that explained everything.

"Still pretty cool," Fred acknowledged.

"Come on, we'll show you the way," Fred offered, starting to walk already and nudging his son to follow. "I can't wait to see those bastards get what's coming to them. Well, the rest anyway," he added with a glance at the dead around them. "Maybe you can help me understand this New York situation better while we walk."

"Sure, just...one minute." Garcia dragged one of the bodies over toward another, then laid it down at an angle, then did the same with another.

"What're you doing, some sort of burial ceremony?" Fred asked.

"No. Creating an arrow." He finished, took one of the blades and jammed it into the ground, hoping it would serve as a marker for his friends should they come by this way. "Done, let's go."

CHAPTER FIVE

The Badlands

The trip out to El Diablo was interesting, hearing Diego talk about all that had happened since Valerie had left them. She had also been chatting with Sandra over the comm device, which she held close now in case they needed to warn New York about any movements they might spot.

Hearing it all from Diego, though, was a totally different beast. She had no idea he had been through so much, and the story of Felix getting hit with the cannonball tore at her heart. He had always been kind to her, and was a damn fine warrior. If it wasn't for him, Diego might have stayed locked up in the Golden City and Cammie might have been killed before Valerie could've gotten to her. She'd only been notified of her predicament when Diego returned with Felix.

Funny how one person could make such a difference.

"Is he going to pull through?" she asked, only then realizing that Diego had kept on going, talking about their other adventures and whatnot.

He laughed. "That big guy? Come on, he wouldn't let something as simple as a cannonball take him out."

"Right. I think even *I* might have to call it quits if a cannonball put a hole in me."

"Nah, you'd never quit. You could be just a head rolling around trying to bite your enemies, and you'd keep on. I'm sure of it."

She laughed this time, nice and loud. "You're ridiculous. Plus, I really hope I would just die at that point. I mean, a head rolling around...that's gotta hurt. All those exposed nerves in the neck and spinal cord area. Ouch."

"We missed you, Val." He stared out at the desert, then pointed to El Diablo so that she could steer the Pod that way. "Sandra says you've been talking a lot about space and what's going on up there. Is that...is that for real?"

She nodded, concentrating on remembering the controls on these Pods and how to lower it without jolting them.

"But, I mean, doesn't that go against the idea of being the Justice Enforcer and all that?"

"Not at all." She figured out the controls and leaned back, pleased to find the Pod moving steadily downward as it advanced on the town. "This whole world has changed so many times in its history, nobody can keep track. Am I right? I mean, for all we know, the gods of ancient Greece could have really been enhanced beings, right? Or maybe aliens were interfering with the Trojan Wars. Maybe King Arthur and that Merlin story had truth to the magic? Arthur could've been a vampire, for all we know."

"What the fuck are you talking about?" he asked, staring at her like she was crazy.

"I mean," she answered with a chuckle, "that this world is unpredictable. There're all those legends, then the crazy talk about some group called the Nazis, which seems even less realistic than all the weird shit I just said...or it would seem that way unless you studied human nature. I don't know. But then the World's Worst Day Ever happens, and for a hundred and fifty years it's just chaos with a few good ones trying to put the world back together. Like that Colonel Walton guy. And now this group I put down in Norway, and this war. It's insane, right?"

"Still not following, but yes."

"Okay, so take all that. Let's say we put an end to it...or not. Does it matter in the slightest if some alien fuckheads come down here and enslave us all or simply destroy the planet once and for all?"

Diego just stared at her, his eyes narrowing.

"The answer's no, Diego. None of that would matter one bit, because it would all be over. We'd all be slaves or dead. No matter how much good we do down here, it doesn't matter in the grand scheme of things, not if we can't keep the attacking forces up there in the stars at bay."

"Damn, when you put it like that..." He shook his head slowly. "And me? Maybe I should—"

"Shut up. Just, stop right there." She held up a hand, not wanting to hear it. "You and Sandra are going to have a baby. Don't you dare talk about leaving that child."

"You said it yourself. What life would that child have if the aliens win?"

He had her there, kind of. "I don't care if I said it or if B.A. herself comes down and tells you you're needed. You even think about leaving Sandra behind to raise that child by herself, about leaving that child fatherless, and I will personally offer up your heart to the aliens. It'll be poisoned so they die after eating it, but they will eat it."

For a long moment he seemed about to explode, but then his tension erupted in a laugh. "Fine. Dammit, Val. You make one hell of an argument for you going, and an even more compelling one for me not to."

"Good. Never talk about it again."

"You think I'd want to do that to Sandra? You think I'd want my child to grow up without me?" He scoffed. "Come on, Val. I'd hope you would have more confidence in me, more faith."

"People have given up their time with their families for far less," she countered with a sigh. "I just can't see you go through that. I couldn't fight knowing that was the case."

"And yet you agreed to let me come out here with you."

She turned to him with a raised eyebrow. "If you think it's going to be that dangerous, if you're worried one bit, I can turn this Pod around right now, mister."

He held up his hands, then nodded to the town. "Too late, we're here."

Sure enough, when she turned back she saw that they had almost landed. The town was right in front of them. Taking back the controls, she maneuvered over to the entrance, then set the Pod down with only a bit of a bump.

"So…" Valerie turned to him before exiting. "All of you, you'll forgive me?"

"For what? Leaving?"

She nodded.

"Yeah, Val. Of course! I mean, you're practically family, so of course we'll miss you."

"And the child?"

"Val, you haven't gone anywhere yet. You don't even know when—"

"Right, I know. But just in case. You'll tell the child all about me, and write me so that I have some way of feeling like I was here?"

"You know Sandra will, and yes, I promise to do my part too."

Valerie breathed out deeply, then opened the door. "Just because I'm committed to doing this doesn't make it easy."

"I bet."

She turned away from him and then mouthed, "Oh, shit!" as a rocket came flying at them. All she could do was grab Diego, then leap up and slide over the Pod. She pinned him under her as the rocket hit the other side of the Pod and exploded, sending the Pod to collide with her body. Flames from the explosion burned hot on her back and the Pod went tumbling over her, but she stood her ground.

When she looked up and Diego wriggled free to see what had just happened, they saw that the Pod was upside down, one side completely singed and dented. The rocket had come from town, and now there was movement.

"Your back," Diego said. "Damn."

She felt the breeze on her skin, but had no time to worry about how badly she'd been hurt. The pain hadn't set in—perhaps out of shock—but she felt the wind on her skin and exposed flesh. It would heal, she figured, and judging by the silhouette of the man with the rocket launcher who was preparing to fire again, they needed to move.

"I see him," Diego grunted, and then he was off, transforming as he ran for the town. His clothes mostly stayed around him, though she heard ripping in a couple places. They were really getting good at figuring out clothes for Weres that would mean less nude moments before and after transforming, but weren't quite at the level of perfection yet.

Valerie wasn't about to sit back and let all the fire be directed toward him, especially not after having just discussed Sandra and the baby.

Skin and flesh ripped as she ran, but she could feel it healing already.

"Why the hell are they firing at us?" she shouted to Diego as she caught up, and then she dove left to try and distract the enemy. No response came since he was in Werecat form and couldn't talk, but the answer hit her as soon as the question had. Of course! They had either been taken over or left.

She wasn't about to waste any time finding out.

Might as well take her chances, staking her speed and skill against some douchebag's aim. She ran straight for the guy, knowing Diego was approaching from a different angle. The man with the rocket launcher freaked, turning from one to the other before finally letting loose. The rocket hit a spot behind her and somewhere between the two. Bullets started flying too, and then she was on the guy, plowing into him so hard that he went flying. His head caved in as it impacted against the brick wall behind him.

She had just turned, ready for more, when she saw a large wolf slam into Diego, and two more coming from the other side.

Dammit, she was sick of killing Weres already.

If she preferred Forsaken instead, she got her wish. As she made a move to intervene, the shooting stopped and a scent hit her from behind, in the building. Forsaken.

She turned back toward them and entered the building, coming face to face with two women and a man. They came at her, eyes glowing red and sharp fangs bared.

Now she was having fun, though it would have been more fun if she could be certain Diego was safe. He was scrappy, so she decided to trust that he was doing just fine.

She blocked a strike and then saw a blade, so she moved around it and caught the woman's arm, bringing the blade back up and into the other woman's eye.

The Forsaken stumbled back, screeching, then pulled the blade out and charged again, bits of eye still on the blade.

"I don't know who you are," Valerie said as she kicked out the man's knee, sidestepped the one-eyed woman's charge, and brought her fist into the third one's throat so that the woman went stumbling back before falling to her knees, "but if you don't tell me what the hell's going on soon, you'll all die."

The Forsaken with the busted knee threw himself at her, trying to bite her calf, but she moved her leg aside and then brought her worn pumas down hard enough to crack his skull.

One of the woman backed off with a horrified expression—the woman with only one eye. "Please, we didn't…"

Whatever she didn't mean to say, Valerie wasn't about to find out, because the other lunged for Valerie's sword. That couldn't be allowed, so Valerie stepped into the lunge, caught the woman by the wrist and pulled the arm around so that it snapped, bone sticking out through skin. Next she shoved the wrist up and into the woman's neck, cutting it open with the woman's own jagged bone.

Done with this, she pulled her sword and made certain of those two by removing their heads. She turned to the third and held the sword to her throat, watching through the torn down walls and broken windows as Diego used his sharp teeth to tear out the last of the wolves' throats.

Several men and women with guns ran forward, though they all looked terrified by what they'd just seen.

Good. Valerie could use that.

"Tell them to surrender," Valerie said, letting the tip of the blade pierce skin. "Hesitate, and I *start* by taking the other eye."

"Shit, shit, shit, everyone back off!" the woman shouted. To Valerie's surprise, they did. She thought she'd have had to convince a few of them, at least.

"You okay?" she asked Diego.

He transformed back to his human form, then glanced around and picked up one of the rifles the Weres had dropped as they transformed.

"I'm good," he replied.

"Good. Now, where were we?" She moved the sword away just enough to let the woman know she could live through this. "Where are the inhabitants of El Diablo? And please don't pretend you are them."

The woman shook her head. "South. We saw them heading south in an airship."

"No shit?" Diego asked.

"And what business did you have here?" Valerie asked. "You must've been nearby for a reason."

"Lady Woo's put out the word to the network, everyone reports in for war," the woman answered. "And extra payment for any that take out this town and one known as El Capitan north a ways. That one...already fell."

Valerie nodded, understanding. "Well, here's what's going to happen. You tell Lady Woo we're coming for her, and that I personally am going to feed on her blood—drain her until there's nothing left. Can you do me that favor if I let you live?"

The woman nodded, her one good eye full of fright.

"Good," Valerie said, then walked out into the light. She glanced back with a taunting smile. "Well, what are you waiting for?"

The woman just stared at her in shock now. "H-how...?"

"You tell your master."

The Forsaken pulled back into the darkness of the building. Valerie turned to the small crowd of men and women, and saw that a couple of them had dropped their weapons.

"Please," one said, stepping forward. A wavy-haired man next to him looked like he was about to shoot the guy, but he paused, considering Valerie and Diego. "You just took down the most powerful creatures they've ever seen," the man continued, "so if you tell these people to switch sides, they might."

"Shut your mouth," the wavy-haired man said.

"These people?" Valerie asked, stepping over to them. "You're not one of them?"

The first man shook his head again, and now that she looked, it was clear there were two groups here. This man was dark skinned and plainly clothed. Half of the others wore black cargo pants and shirts, including the wavy-haired man.

"Let me guess," she asked the dark-skinned man. "You're from the other town that was taken over?"

He nodded, cautiously glancing over at the others. "They forced us to join. How many others in this army of Lady Woo's were forced, I wonder?"

"That's enough!" the wavy-haired man said, lifting his rifle to shoot. Valerie, naturally, couldn't let that happen. In a flash she was at his side, moving the rifle so that when the man's finger pulled the trigger, it was aimed into his mouth.

He fell instantly.

"There you go," Valerie told the group. "Any of you want to follow this man's lead, you're welcome to it. Anyone on my side will hold down El Diablo for me and its inhabitants until you hear otherwise. Am I clear?"

"And if we want to join *her* to return to Lady Woo?" another one of the cargo pants-wearers asked.

Valerie laughed. "Diego, what do you think? Should we let some of these people run off to join our enemy in the assault on your home? On the very city where your pregnant wife waits for your return?"

Diego didn't even answer, simply shot the man three times— once in the head, twice in the chest.

"I'll take that as 'no, we won't allow that,'" Valerie said, nodding. She didn't like playing the ruthless leader, but she was pretty sure this didn't qualify as anything other than stopping bad people and protecting those she loved.

"South?" she asked, glancing around again.

The dark-skinned man nodded. "Just...look for a blimp. It wasn't going very fast."

"Great. Now, can you point out everyone who was fully on Lady Woo's side before my arrival?" She waited as the man did so, then addressed those he had pointed out. "Decision time, ladies and gentlemen. Surrender to these people, or see what happens next."

They all surrendered.

"And the vampire?" the man asked.

"She needs to deliver the message. If she tries to hurt anyone, feel free to shoot her and remove her head. Otherwise, when night comes, let her be on her way." She paused, considering. "I'm guessing they came at night?"

The man shook his head and motioned to long poles with cloths attached. "They make us carry that, on pain of death, while we're on the move."

"You could just throw it down and they would die, right?"

He shrugged, wincing at how easy that thought was. "Maybe, but they'd still kill us. The Weres, I mean."

"Sure. Just something to think about next time."

He gave her a hopeful smile. "It's not common to say it was a pleasure to meet someone and actually mean it, but in this case I really do. It was a pleasure. Name's Tony."

"Valerie," she replied, and shook his hand. "Let's ride, Diego."

Diego turned to her with an expression like she was crazy. "In what?"

"We'll get the Pod up, don't worry."

"You all need help?" Tony asked.

She nodded. "We've got it."

As they walked off, Diego asked, "Are you sure about this? They likely know where Woo is, right?"

"First friends, then the enemy," Valerie replied. "Because if a friend dies I could never live with it, but if an enemy lives one more day I can just kill her the next."

He chuckled. "I like your philosophy."

When they reached the Pod she got under the side and heaved, and it flipped back up with relative ease. Diego whistled and smiled in awe.

"Stop standing there with your mouth open," she told him, "and hop in so we can go get some more blood on our hands."

47

CHAPTER SIX

The Badlands

Cammie smelled the blood before the others; all but Royland. A glance showed him to be alert, eyeing the nearby hills as if expecting an ambush.

"There," Cammie whispered, pointing to a glimmer in the distance. As they approached, it became clear it was a car, completely rusted over and broken off in places. The glimmer was actually from a long knife stuck halfway into the ground next to one of the bodies.

Micky whistled. "Your Army pal did a number here, that's for sure."

"I thought you said these guys were badass," Cammie commented. "They're looking a bit less intimidating right now."

"Being dead will do that," Arturo replied. "Plus, I'm thinking the term badass means something else entirely when someone's up against you and your friends."

"To be clear," Royland interjected, "Garcia isn't a Were or a vampire. He just knows how to handle himself."

Micky nodded in acknowledgment, and they started moving in the direction of the arrow.

"That Colonel Walton character Garcia always goes on about must really be something," Micky stated after a few minutes of walking. "If every one of his fighters is anything like Garcia, I'd feel pretty damn sorry for any of his enemies."

"Last I'd heard, our pal Sandra had given the Colonel a call and some more of his troops might be heading over to help end all this. Right now, our enemy is his enemy."

"Well then, I feel glad I chose the right side."

Their journey brought them past an old strip mall that had somehow only fallen apart in a few places at the edges. It was clearly being occupied by some of the crazier inhabitants of the Badlands.

"This isn't our group," Micky stated, nodding onward. "Best avoid them, if possible."

As they passed, the group stared at them, more coming out to join the first few until there were about twenty in all. One wore a headdress of straw and another had two umbrellas. He twirled one around, picking his mustache as he watched them pass.

"When the fighting breaks out, where do they stand?" Royland asked.

"They're more like a pack of wild dogs than anything else," Arturo replied. "If our enemy can get them out and point them in the right direction, they'll fight us. But they're just as likely to turn on Lady Woo before the fighting even starts."

"Someone needs to put them out of their misery," Micky noted. "But we don't want to risk the lives it might cost."

Cammie shook her head. "I used to run with groups like these. People thought *I* was crazy, but look at me now."

"You're with me," Royland stated. "You must be batshit insane."

She laughed. "Ain't that the truth."

Arturo and Micky exchanged nervous looks, but kept on. They were glad to leave the wackos behind them, and soon were descending into a basin of dead grass and old torn-apart vehicles with a hill on the far side.

"Look lively," Royland warned, sniffing the air. "We have company."

"More of those crazies?" Micky asked, turning to the hill.

"Doesn't seem like it, no."

"That's what I thought. Look there." Micky gestured to the hill and an area where the old junk had been piled up. "Must be one of their regular haunts."

"And at this point, I imagine they've seen us." Cammie unslung her rifle just in case, but then had a thought. The easiest way to get their attention was to lure them out. "I'm going in."

"They'll slaughter you," Arturo said, full of shock.

"Not Cammie, they won't," Royland argued. "But still, I'm not sure I follow."

She smiled, enjoying being the one with the plan. "You all work your way around the sides; see if there's any sign of Garcia. When I get up there, we'll see what they do. They take a shot at me, I charge in and kill 'em all. They make some other move, we all do the same. Hell, maybe we'll get lucky and find out Garcia already took care of the situation."

"Right, that sounds like our kind of lucky," Royland replied with a chuckle.

"Well, based on what we've seen on the way over," Micky stated, "I wouldn't be so surprised."

"Where do you want me?" Royland asked.

"As close as you can get without being seen," she replied. "Ready to jump in should shit hit the fan."

She approached on foot alone, hands held up to show she was unarmed.

She knew the others were sneaking around, so when the woman coming at her holding a rifle started shouting, her heart-beat barely increased at all.

"You want a problem, keep approaching," the lady shouted. "Who the fuck are you, and what do you want?"

Cammie paused, hands out at her sides. "To hire you."

The woman wore the brown and gray clothes of the corpses they had found on the way over, so there was no doubt they were in the right place.

With a tilt of her head, she lowered the rifle slightly and asked, "Who is it you want targeted?"

It was impossible not to smile as Cammie replied, "Your group, actually. I want to hire you to walk back in there, kill the rest of them, and then wander out here for your payment."

"That'd have to be a mighty fine payment," the woman said, lifting the rifle again to aim it.

"Ohhh, I got confused, see? I was thinking of payback for what you did to Pops."

Now the woman's eyes went wide and she started shooting. It was go time.

Glad she had worn her stretchy clothes for this occasion, Cammie ran forward, transforming into wolf mode as she moved. There was no reason to hold back on these people. It wasn't like the north, where she had hoped to win the enemy to her side. Here it was about teaching a lesson to others while crushing any evil remaining in this place.

While she had once fought out here as a young woman intent on escaping to freedom and caring only about her own survival, those days were long gone.

The woman with the rifle backed away, eyes wide as she screamed. More gunshots rang out, but no way was Cammie going to give them the satisfaction of hitting her. As she dodged using her full Were speed, a snarl sounded nearby, followed by a scream and then another.

Royland had struck, and the surrounding gunshots were redirected toward him as she crushed the woman's larynx with her powerful jaws. She kept moving, now aware of shooting from her right. It wasn't at her, though. It was at the city. Micky and the others were on the move.

———

"What the hell was that?" Fred asked, perking up at the sound of gunshots.

Garcia listened, then moved up to the ledge and looked over, pulling back with a smile. "My friends are here."

They had been working their way around the hills to get at their target from the back, but now that seemed unnecessary.

"On me!" Garcia yelled as he stood and charged around the hill.

The other two were close behind, though he was vaguely aware of Fred shouting at his son to stay back out of trouble.

Each step seemed to slide down the gravely dirt; his knees wanted to buckle. He needed to get down there though, in part because it was his friends fighting and he saw it as his responsibility to never let any of his friends get hurt—not on his watch. But more than that, it was because he had gotten here first! *This was his kill, dammit.*

He watched as more fighters streamed out of the blimp that had set down just out of firing range, many of them easily distinguishable by their large size and leather. It would have made him smile, if not for the urge to kill and the rush of adrenalin that pushed him forward with a battle cry on his lips.

Gravel gave way to solid dirt as he reached the bottom. Springing around piles of crushed metal, he came face to face with one of the warriors who looked to have been sneaking around to catch Cammie and the others by surprise. Three shots took him down, and then two more appeared.

These ones were quick, slicing at him and dodging his blows. Enough so that he started to understand where they had gotten their reputation. A dodge left met him with a kick to the face, and he'd only managed to back up in time to avoid a knife thrust because Fred had appeared and shouted, "Watch out!"

One of the fighters moved to intercept Fred and his son, but Garcia couldn't have that.

He decided to try an old trick from his training days with the Colonel. As the next strike came he stepped into it, smacking the blade aside with his rifle and then headbutting his opponent. Honor in hand to hand had never been his thing—especially when lives were at stake—so he didn't even let his opponent recover before blasting him full of holes.

The other fighter and Fred were locked in combat, but a stone thrown by Eddie Jr. caused the fighter to pull back for a moment, and that was all Garcia needed. A shot to the leg and one more to the chest put him on the ground. Once the man was down, Fred grabbed his knife and finished the job.

Garcia was about to move on when Eddie Jr. looked past him, pointing, and asked, "What's that?"

Turning, Garcia stumbled in surprise at the sight of a Pod approaching from the left of the blimp. A Pod just like the ones they had in New York.

"Reinforcements," he said, smiling. He had a good idea of who would be on that Pod, and looked forward to seeing her again. "Come on, let's take out as many of them as we can before she arrives."

He charged, moving toward the opening in the hill nearby.

"She?" Fred asked as he joined the charge.

"You'll see, buddy." Garcia laughed. "You'll see."

It should have come as no surprise to Valerie that she was once again flying straight into a fight. She had hoped to have some time with Cammie, to ask what had happened in Norway and make sure they were all doing fine, but that would have to wait.

Sandra had mostly filled her in anyway, and it sounded like everything had gone smoothly for them.

The dead Weres in Valerie's wake showed it hadn't gone quite so well for everyone back there. Not the evil dickheads, anyway.

Now it was time to do some more good for the world.

"Ready, buddy?" she asked as they touched down and she threw open the dented door.

"Always," Diego replied, ducking out and transforming as he moved.

Valerie darted forward to scan the situation. There were the men in leather Diego had told her about, and they were on her side. Someone was screaming near a hole in the mountain, so that must be where Cammie had run off to—and Royland, most likely. He probably would have gotten out of the sun as fast as possible, enjoying the opportunity to not worry about death by sunlight.

If that was where her friends were, she might as well join them.

Guns were going off here and there, but mostly there were only the sounds of bodies being slammed into the ground or men screaming as knives did their damage. Valerie tore through two fighters trying to take on a large man, slamming them together so that their heads caved in. Then she was at the cave entrance, turning at the last moment to send a bullet into another attacker's forehead—the idiot had thought he could sneak up on her. A thought hit her that she might want to *push* fear and put a stop to this, but she knew it would have an effect on her friends and allies too, and didn't want to put them through the equivalent of a mental barrage of arrows.

Ducking into the tunnels in this mountain, she had to wonder if it had been dug out since the great collapse or had been around before. She turned one corner to find a tunnel with old lights and walls paneled with sheets of the scrap metal from outside. Still, it had a fairly militaristic look about it.

Everything down here smelled of blood and piss.

A woman in a leather jacket was crawling toward her, the jacket now hanging in shreds and blood pouring out of her. There was no way she would make it without help, so Valerie paused. She hated this. It had been a while since she'd had to offer someone her blood to heal. With Sandra, back in the day, it had been as much about loyalty and devotion as healing and staying young, and even then she tried not to do it too often. The last thing she wanted was for her only friend to become addicted to the stuff. But if she were going to make allies here, a bit of pain to save a life would be a good way to start.

So it was with only a slight hesitation that Valerie knelt, bit into her wrist, and let the woman drink from her. The skin healed quickly and then Valerie was up, a hand on the woman's shoulder.

"You should survive this, and you owe me a beer," she said as she moved down the tunnel.

There was no room for proper swordplay down here so she kept it sheathed, instead pulling the pistol she had strapped to her thigh as she used to. Holding it with both hands, she turned the next corner already prepared, thanks to her keen sense of smell.

BAM! BAM!

Two shots and the enemy fell, but the next corner brought her a view of another taking on three of the El Diablo fighters. *Damn, this guy was good.* Too bad for him he couldn't compete with a vampire.

"Stand back," Valerie demanded, voice firm and not allowing for argument. Her eyes glowed red as she darted forward, picking up the man by the neck and swatting his knives aside with her free hand.

She decided this would be a great time to replenish the blood she had given up, even though she wasn't sure she needed to with Michael's blood flowing through her. On top of that was the idea that the El Diablo fighters might be inspired by knowing they had an all-powerful vampire on their side. *The show must go on, after all*, she thought as she sank her fangs into the screaming man's throat.

Blood gushed, tasting like rusted metal and a hint of burnt sausage. When she was done she flung him to the ground, still alive, and said, "He's yours."

The others moved in to finish him off while she continued down the tunnel.

A roar sounded and she paused. Sure enough, there was the scent of a Were, one she recognized. Picking up the pace, she worked through a maze of tunnels, some so low that she had to duck, and came out in a space that had clearly been used as an armory and had three doors leading off it.

Cammie was in the middle in human form, taking on three fighters. Valerie was about to move in and help, but the Were was handling herself quite nicely. She was quick, her reflexes almost as fast as a vampire's, and while she took a couple of cuts across the torso and arms, she would heal. The pain just seemed to push her to go faster and harder, and she soon sent two to their deaths. Only when she turned and saw Valerie did she pause, giving the opponent the upper hand.

His strike was moving right for her throat, but Valerie couldn't allow that. She took three quick steps and grabbed the attacking arm, twisting so that the blade fell as the shoulder joint dislocated. Next she stepped behind the man, put her claws to his throat, and tore it open.

He collapsed in a gurgling shriek of pain and was gone.

"Oh my God," Cammie declared, stepping back, hand to her chest.

"No, just me." Valerie glanced around, checking to see that they were clear.

"How the hell'd you find us?" Cammie asked. "Of course, I'm glad you did, I just… Wow."

"There were others at El Diablo who saw you leave, then we spotted the airship, and, yeah—not too difficult from there. I see you've gotten yourself into a bit of a mess."

"Think so?" Cammie glanced at the three dead warriors in the room with them. "Made a mess, yes."

Valerie froze at the scent of a vampire, but then recognized it. "Don't attack, Royland. It's me—Val."

Royland came around the corner, hesitant at first, and then smiled widely.

"Where the hell did you go off to?" he asked, then paused, and with a glance over his shoulder sprinted off and killed a man. When he came back he said, "I mean, shit, Val! You could've left us a message. At least Garcia had the good thought of leaving the bodies in an arrow so we'd know where he went. You didn't even bother to do that."

She laughed and shook her head. "Hey, I went looking for you all too. At least you could've stayed in town for a bit before taking off."

"Wait, you went back there after we left?" Cammie asked. "And now look at us. All back together again for one last glorious battle."

"I doubt it will be the last," Valerie replied. "Maybe the last *here*."

"For us it will," Cammie said, nodding to Royland. "After this is over, we mean to settle down for as long as the world allows."

"You won't go into space?"

Cammie cringed. "God, no. What the hell makes you think I'd want to do that?"

"Oh, I don't know. Maybe the idea that you could learn what's out there, fight for the survival of the human race... The list goes on."

"Good luck convincing her," Royland interjected. "She wants a dog."

"A dog?" Valerie stared at her friend. This was not the Cammie she had met when she first arrived in New York.

Cammie shrugged.

"And you, Royland?" Valerie asked. "I suppose I already know the answer."

"You do."

"She's got you whipped, huh?"

He just laughed at that. "Hell yes, she does."

Valerie assessed the three doors, but Cammie smiled and shook her head.

"Already got 'em." Cammie motioned to the three bodies on the floor. "Far as I can tell these were the last three, unless any escaped out a back way."

"Come on, then." Valerie started leading the way out. "We'd better check on our friends out there and see how they're holding up."

The trio made their way to the entrance, Royland grumbling about moving around in sunlight and wanting sleep as he put on his mask.

Walking back into daylight after being in those tunnels would've likely made others cringe, but Valerie's eyes adjusted immediately. She looked around and was glad to find the El Diablo people there waiting, Diego in their midst.

"Took you long enough," the werecat said with a smirk. "We did all the dirty work while you were playing hide and seek."

"Am I going crazy, or did Sandra actually let you come out here?" Royland asked when he saw him.

"Hey, she doesn't control me," Diego replied, shaking hands with the vampire.

"Right—don't think of it as control. That helps you stay saner, I bet. Too bad I lost my marbles years ago, or that'd be something I'd have to worry about to."

"Enough, you two," Cammie interjected, then quickly introduced Valerie to the big man named Micky and his buddy

Arturo before saying, "How about we focus on the mission at hand?"

"These bastards took out Pops," Micky stated. "Now they've paid for it, but that doesn't change the fact that Lady Woo was behind it and has to pay too."

"Right, and there's the whole 'war against her' thing," Cammie replied. She turned to Valerie and explained that Diego and Garcia had gone up against Lady Woo not long ago, and she was the one leading the war against New York.

"So the plan," Royland interjected, "was to go after her. Bite off the snake's head, if you will."

"Only problem with that plan," a man said, coming up to them with Garcia and a boy, "is that Lady Woo's going to be holed up real good. You get to her, you might as well kill off the rest of them too, just end the war."

"And you would be?" Valerie asked.

"This is Fred," Garcia answered for him, then gave her a handshake. "Thought I'd catch you when I first got to New York. You're as elusive as a jackrabbit."

"I had business to attend to up north," she replied, glad to see him. "It couldn't wait."

He nodded, then added, "Fred here was a messenger from Lady Woo to this lovely group of corpses."

"On your side now, though," Fred replied, holding up his hands to show he wasn't a threat. "Garcia here's been talking you all up, and I gotta say, might be more than just me and my son would switch sides if you spread the message right."

"And how would we do that?" Valerie asked.

"Keep with the plan to move in stealthy, but set me and some others loose to persuade some of 'em we know we can trust. We see who's with us, you wait to kill anyone en masse, and we go from there."

Valerie pursed her lips, considering this. "You think there are enough of them who would turn on her?"

"I think there are a lot of people who are scared, who don't know what they're getting into. I think these same people would be willing to at least listen."

"I could go with him," Garcia offered. "If anyone tries something, we fight our way back to you all, then raise hell."

"Meanwhile we see about assassinating Lady Woo and her top people," Valerie added, liking the plan already. "It won't stop people from fighting, but it *will* cause confusion, which, combined with you convincing at least some of them to switch sides, will throw them for a loop."

"Exactly," Fred replied.

"I like you, Fred." Valerie turned to the others. "If anyone wants to seek safety, we can get the airship back to New York with you on it, but we need to know now. No tucking tail and running in the middle of a fight."

"My son," Fred offered. "If anything happened to Eddie Jr. I'd never forgive myself."

"What?" Eddie Jr. protested. "No, you can't be serious. I can fight, Dad!"

"You can, but you won't."

A couple of the former inhabitants of El Diablo stepped forward, asking to go too.

"Right." Valerie counted seven, including the boy. "Here's what we do: we escort them back, some of us in the Pod, the rest in the airship. Get them to New York, then put our plan into play."

The rest agreed and they set off for the airship and Pod, prepared to make their move.

CHAPTER SEVEN

New York

Sandra was still pissed at Diego for leaving her. While she understood it, understanding something was a long way from liking it.

And she wasn't the only one not happy.

The citizens of New York were growing restless, that much was clear. Sandra hopped to the wall in a Pod, watching the demonstration. The protesters had all lined up near the walls, demanding to know what was happening. If it got much worse violence would break out in the city, which was the main thing they were trying to avoid.

They found one of the extended areas of the wall made for landing the Pod and touched down. The soldier accompanying her asked her to hold for a moment while he made sure they were safe.

"I'll be fine," she replied, but when he glanced back at her, eyes drifting to her belly, she sighed and added, "but if you must."

She often forgot that it wasn't just her to think about anymore. Even if she wanted to be cavalier, another life was depending on her. It annoyed her no end that this was all she seemed to think about nowadays, but when you had someone living and growing inside you it was hard to let your mind wander too far away.

A knock on the Pod signaled it was clear, so she emerged and nodded to the soldier. He stood with the butt-end of his rifle in his shoulder, muzzle down but ready in case there should be trouble. Whether that trouble would be from outside or within, she didn't want to ask.

With everything that had gone on in New York, she wanted to believe the people were moving on from days of violence. That they had changed. No, she *insisted* on believing it.

A glance at the demonstrators gave her a moment's doubt, but then she turned to the ruins and desolate land beyond New York and sighed. No matter what happened here they were better off than being out there; that was certain.

Despite the dreariness of it all, the descending sun cast long shadows across the ruins of what had once been surrounding cities and rippled gold across the water. It was, in its own disturbing way, quite beautiful.

Movement caught her attention in the ruins to the southwest. Her heart thumped extra hard as she considered that this could be them—the enemy. The war could start right now.

But as she watched, it became clear this was just one individual—someone who had lost their mind long ago, most likely. How many of them wandered around out there—lost, barely surviving—she had no idea, but wished there was something to be done about them.

Not wanting to go down that whirlpool of depressing thought, she glanced at the man she was waiting to see. Jackson.

"They've heard, you know," Jackson said as he approached, stopping at a point where they had secured large guns to the walls. He held the handle of one of them, sighting down the barrel as if about to take on the enemy, and then turned back to her with a serious expression. "The people of New York, they know there's danger ahead."

"I think that's kinda obvious, and why we're here," she replied, irritation dripping from her voice. She wasn't a child who needed her hand held during this process. "We need to get them away from the walls and back inside where it's safe."

"Will it be?" he asked. "Safe, I mean?"

At that she shrugged. "Maybe nowhere's safe, but I have to believe we've trained the soldiers well enough. We have Weres, we have vampires. We have the city walls. There's no reason to think we can't hold our own in this war."

"And we have Valerie," he added, turning back to look at the horizon. "Or at least, she's out there somewhere."

"Maybe putting a stop to all this before we have to do anything."

"Yes, that's a possibility. Or maybe running off, abandoning us."

Sandra frowned. "I thought you were moving on."

"This isn't about me. You can't deny that she tends to pursue one problem after another. How do you know she hasn't seen something else out there, some other great evil, and decided to take care of it, leaving us behind?"

"You know what?" Sandra shook her head, making a *tsk* sound with her tongue. "It's sad you don't have more faith in us. In her."

"You're saying I'm wrong?"

"No, I'm saying that if she found another problem out there I'd trust her judgment. I wouldn't doubt for a moment that she would be making the right choice for the safety of humanity. Plus, like I said, we can fend for ourselves."

He scrunched his nose, eyebrows furrowed, then looked away.

"You know I'm right," Sandra insisted. "Personal matters shouldn't cloud your opinion of her."

"What do you want from me?"

"The people listen to you. Respect you." Sandra turned to look at the protesters. "We need to find out who among them can fight, and get the rest underground. Maybe to the old hideouts, the underground ones."

CHAPTER EIGHT

Outside New York

New York rose up before Valerie in her Pod. Micky was sitting beside her, with Diego, Cammie, and Royland in the back. The blimp carrying Micky's buddies plus Garcia, Fred, and Eddie Jr. floated behind them.

Valerie had the comm device next to her as she flew, and had just buzzed Sandra.

"Val?" The woman's voice came through clearly. "About time. Is Diego okay?"

Snickers came from the back as Diego said, "I'm right here, dear. All my bullet holes will have healed by the time we see each other. Don't worry, I'll be as handsome as ever."

"That's not funny," Sandra snapped.

"He's fine." Valerie shot Diego a glare. "In fact, we're on our way back, but not for long. We're dropping off the people who want to lay low and then some of us are going back out there."

"What? What for?"

"I'll fill you in when we see you. Where will you be?"

"The western wall." There was a silence before she added, "And Diego's plan?"

"Wow, she's actually asking instead of just commanding you?" Micky whispered to Diego, earning him an elbow in the ribs.

"Dear," Diego leaned forward to talk into the comm, "I'll go where I'm most needed. You want me at your side, say the word."

"But we could use him out here," Valerie interjected. "I get your position, Sandra. It's your call. Just know he'd be valuable on the outside."

"Forget me and my pregnancy, huh?" Sandra sighed. "Fine. Take him."

"Don't get all dramatic," Valerie countered. "You know I've got his six, so what's the big deal?"

"Maybe we could chat about this when you don't have a Pod full of people listening in?"

"Fine." Valerie glared at the others as if it were their fault she had to cut this short. She was starting to see the outline of the city, so she finished the call. For a moment she debated whether she was being greedy or not, but the point was that they needed to do whatever they could to put an end to this war as quickly as possible…even if that meant keeping two lovebirds apart for another day or two.

Especially when doing so meant fewer lives lost, preferably on both sides.

"When we go out there we need to know that we're with real fighters, real warriors," Valerie stated, glancing back at Micky. "Can we count on your people for that?"

"You think we've survived in the Badlands as long as we have and don't know how to fight?"

"I'll take that as a yes."

"You should," Diego chimed in. "They held their own when we retreated to the city. These guys and gals are badass."

"Aw, thanks, little guy." Micky laughed.

"They're not very bright, but badass," Diego corrected.

"Not very bright?" Cammie asked.

"He just proved that by calling me 'little guy,'" Diego explained.

Micky laughed at this too. "Hey, I'm not denying that you could take me in a fight. I've seen you at work. That doesn't change your stature."

"It's all relative, right? Take, for example, your belly. I think you're right—relative to you, I'm tiny. At least three of me could fit in that gut of yours."

"Now you're just being mean," Micky grumbled, leading to the others chuckling.

"When we get there," Valerie started, changing the subject back to the mission, "I want to touch down, let them off, and get moving again."

"Might not be as easy as that," Cammie replied. She touched Valerie's shoulder and pointed out the window.

Her words made sense instantly as Valerie saw shapes moving on the ground. Then there was a burst of light and...

PING! PING!

"Shots fired!" Valerie announced, swerving the Pod to evade the gunfire and get a better view of what was below them.

Only now it was an explosion of bursts of light—shots were being fired by hundreds of guns. She pulled up and to the left, getting out of there, and then circled back toward the blimp.

"*Open fire!*" she shouted, and a moment later the windows were down and she and Royland were shooting into the night, trying to take out as many as they could. There were just too many, though, and it became clear the airship wasn't going to make it with all those holes in it.

It was also clear that their attackers were moving toward New York, but Valerie preferred to deal with one problem at a time.

"Keep their focus away from the airship!" Valerie commanded and pulled the Pod around, making circles around the airship and unleashing a fury of shots as her companions fired downward.

Bursts were coming from the airship too as Garcia and others returned fire on the attackers below, but somehow the enemy had managed to hit all sides of the airship.

"Dammit!" Cammie shouted. "The city's too far. They won't make it."

Valerie was about to argue, but she observed that the balloon on the airship was already deflating, the ship losing altitude.

She glanced at the ground below them and saw a spot where old buildings formed a bit of a wall with an old train yard beyond it. They would land there.

Pulling hard on the controls, Valerie steered the Pod directly toward the front of the airship.

"You're going to crash!" Micky shouted, bracing himself while the others continued to shoot.

"Have faith," Valerie replied. "I'm only going to crash a little."

"WHAT?"

"Just to nudge them in the right direction. Brace yourselves for impact!"

Half the Pod was screaming, Cammie was laughing, and the explosions and gunshots continued.

They hit with a thud and pushed the airship toward the railyard.

"Come on, girl!" Valerie shouted as they fell more and more, the ship close to hitting the top of a half-collapsed building.

It scraped across and then they were clear. The gunfire couldn't reach them anymore as they dropped behind the rest of the ruins and moved toward the old trains.

"Check your ammo," Valerie said as she aimed for a clear spot to land. "Now it gets dangerous."

CHAPTER NINE

New York

Sandra had just put away her comm device when the shooting started in the distance. At first she thought it might be a random skirmish, but her heart froze at what she saw—the airship and Pod in the sky taking bright bursts of gunfire from below. Both ships started to return fire, but then, to her horror, the airship went down.

Her first instinct was to scream. Diego was out there, and she saw the Pod following the airship. It wasn't clear if the Pod had been hit. Her second instinct, which she acted on, was to pull the comm device back out and start calling Valerie frantically, but there was no response.

Of course, she realized as she put it away. They were likely fighting for their lives right now. There was no time to answer the comm.

As she watched she saw movement in the distance and more shots moving toward the downed airship, and then it hit her. This army was coming here! They were en route to New York already, but had been distracted by the airship and Pod.

"Soldier!" she shouted to the night guard who had just come on shift. "Sound the alarm. They're here."

He had been watching the action too, so he didn't need to ask what she meant before taking off.

It was go-time, and that meant she didn't belong up here. A stray bullet or shrapnel to the belly and she would never forgive herself.

As she turned, she saw Davies moving along the wall in her direction.

"I didn't know you were out here," she stated.

"Making the rounds, checking on the soldiers. You saw what happened?"

She nodded. "Better than saw, I was on the comm device with Valerie and Diego, saw the shooters take them down. They have reinforcements out there."

"You're wondering if we can send a team out?" He considered this, then shook his head. "We have Val, Diego, Cammie, Royland, and Garcia out there already. They're the best team there is. Anyone else would just be at risk."

"My thoughts as well," she replied. "I'm going to check on the people underground. Ensure they're secure, at ease."

"Someone has to, and honestly…I'm glad it's you."

"Oh?"

He shrugged. "In my mind, dealing with people like that in times like these, well, that takes more courage than standing on this wall any day."

Nodding, she moved to the steps, but paused to glance back and say, "If you see an opportunity, take it. If Diego's harmed, I'll go out there on my own and kill every last one of them."

More shots sounded in the distance, but she forced her way down the steps one foot at a time. Every instinct in her said to grab a rifle and run to her man, but the reality of the situation was that she wasn't Valerie. She was Sandra, and knew her strengths and weaknesses. Right now it was about ensuring the safety of New York's people.

But she had one stop to make on the way.

The city was restless, faces appearing at windows and men stepping out through their doors with various weapons. As she walked, she noticed some of them following. No, not following—going in the same direction. When she reached Capital Square, she understood.

She had come to find Jackson, but so had they.

"We have our little army," Jackson said, seeing her.

The others were gathering behind him in a half-circle, preparing to defend the city, and Sandra had to admit it was a sight worth seeing. Still, it raised a question or two in her mind.

"Something tells me you didn't just cobble these fighters together at the last minute."

His expression gave nothing away, but a twinkle in his eyes told her all she needed to know.

"Uh huh," she said, continuing. "I came here to see if you were doing your part, and I rest assured you are." She paused. "But when it's over?"

"I have my followers. They're ready to fight if I see injustice. It's nothing more than that."

"Good," she replied. "In a world like this we couldn't expect anything less. But...promise to at least discuss what you see as injustice before taking matters into your own hands?"

"Agreed."

With that she made for the underground tunnels. She had once spent time there with Valerie and Diego preparing a siege on Enforcer HQ, but now she would be joining others to lay low as New York was attacked.

She would have to trust the city's defense to Valerie, Cammie, Royland, Diego, Davies, Jackson, and the rest.

When she moved aside a piece of plywood at an old subway

station, she had to ignore the smell of the place. It reminded her of rotten potatoes, her pregnancy adding to the level of nausea.

It wasn't so bad once she had gone down the steps, and she was relieved to see Clara there waiting. This girl had quickly grown to be one of Sandra's favorites, especially since she was always willing to bring her a treat or check in on her when everyone else was off worrying about city defenses.

"I was hoping you'd be down soon," Clara said. "When I heard the shooting, I figured it was time."

"Let's check on the others," Sandra replied, wrapping an arm around the younger woman and walking with her through the dim tunnel. "How are the children?"

"More have been streaming in, especially in the last few minutes."

"And I imagine Platea's off worrying about Garcia. He'll be fine, he always is."

"She's been mostly helping to organize," Clara replied. "But, yes, to keep her mind off it all."

"We'll need to close off the entrances when the fighting really starts, be ready to set up our own defenses if they breach the walls."

"Hey, former pirate here! If they get down here, they'll be in for a rude awakening."

Sandra laughed. "Don't discount me yet either. I pack a mean punch."

"You can fight?"

"I was trained by militaristic vampires. Meaning, yes." She noticed the glance down at the protruding belly. "Right... I'll try to avoid it as much as possible."

"Probably smart," Clara replied.

They turned into a hallway that Sandra recognized from the last time she had been down there. Artificial lighting gave it a yellow hue, and the hum of frightened talk created an eerie feeling. Glancing around at the eyes of the children there, she saw she wasn't alone in feeling this.

If they were going to move on after the fighting was done, this state of terror would have to be long gone.

"Everyone, if I can have your attention?" She waved a hand and motioned them over, and soon people were packed into the tunnel. "Who here remembers what it was like before? Under Commander Strake?"

A few nods from the crowd.

"And who here has any idea what it's like outside of these walls? In the Badlands?"

"It's a shithole," a man replied.

"Yes, but...*language*," she replied with a nod at a group of children nearby. "The point is, none of you want to go back to that. None of you want this city to fall into the hole of feces this man so eloquently described. We are not the Badlands, and never will be. We are the people of New York, and we will survive this."

Several people mumbled in agreement.

"Be strong for your children, parents. And children, be strong for your parents. There's nothing more encouraging than when a mother looks down and sees her little one being braver than she feels. Likewise, if the warriors of this city see us holding our heads high, they'll know we're not afraid. They'll know we have faith in them, and that no matter what, we won't let this city fall. Am I right?"

"Yeah!" Bronson called, his kids laughing around him.

"I'd rather be out there fighting," one of his sons said, the one she had been told was a Were.

She chuckled and shook her head. "Many of us would be, but we have a front line. Let them do their jobs, and we'll stay here to protect those who need us."

The boy nodded.

"Why's this happening?" a woman asked, her thick eyebrows

amplifying the glare she was giving Sandra. "I thought this was your job—to keep the city under control. Safe."

"And we are," Sandra replied. "We have forces beyond the walls working to take out our enemies as we speak. I've put a call out to a certain colonel out west, Colonel Walton, and he's promised to send some soldiers to help us out. To form an alliance—and that's what this is. This is the formation of the greatest alliance any of us have seen in our lifetimes. We're going to be able to sit back and enjoy peace after this—I'm certain of it —but before any period of peace comes strife. The land will be our Eden, but not until we rid it of the serpent who is Lady Woo."

"Fine," the woman replied. "But that doesn't explain why you talk like one of those old-school recruiting posters."

The others laughed and Sandra found herself smiling.

"Blame that on Valerie."

"The dead lady?" the woman asked. "The one they say was…" she glanced around, debating whether she should say it in front of the children, and then lowered her voice, "a vampire?"

Nervous glances followed.

"A vampire…" Sandra considered the question. There was so much to it, after all. The idea that the UnknownWorld should be kept secret, for one. The fact that Valerie had faked her own death. That was her secret to deal with, but it had been to trick the CEOs, their enemy at the time, so that they wouldn't lead any more attacks on the city in an attempt to find her.

Still, it wasn't Sandra's place to reveal the truth—not yet.

"Valerie was like a sister to me, and I was raised across the ocean with her, trained in a militaristic fashion. She was always talking like this, inspiring others. As I hope I have done tonight, at least to a small degree."

"You've got my vote," Clara called from the back of the room.

"Vote of confidence?" Sandra asked.

"Whatever vote you want," the girl replied. "When this is over the people of New York will need a representative, after all."

74

Sandra had been a follower so much of her life before coming here, the idea of being a voice for the people in any way took her a second to come to grips with. When more people chimed in with agreement, she smiled and said, "One step at a time."

"At least say you won't dismiss the idea," Bronson requested.

She nodded, an action that was met by several cheers.

"Okay, okay. I came here to ensure we were all ready for what's about to come our way, not pitch myself for a leadership position."

"Which is exactly what makes you perfect for it," Bronson countered. "Plus, you're already on the council. No reason to shy away from what's clearly your destiny."

She laughed, but saw he was serious. They were all serious.

"I'll think about it," she promised. "*After* this war is over."

The others agreed and went back to whatever they had been doing before the impromptu meeting. Some were checking on food supplies as more boxes of fruits and crackers were delivered. Others would be taking up guard positions and blockading doors.

"That was some speech," Bronson said, working his way through the crowd with his three children. Even the Were boy had looked a bit scared, but didn't now. "We just wanted to remind you that we're here if you need us."

One hand went to the pistol at his side and the other rested on the Were boy's shoulder.

"Stay close," Sandra replied. "It's going to be an interesting night."

Sandra was about to move on and check on another section of the underground hideout, when her comm device went off. Her hands shook with excitement as she pulled it out, thinking it must be Valerie and Diego, but it was an unrecognized name. Someone called Espinoza.

"This is Sandra," she said after moving into a side tunnel that wasn't as crowded. First the sound of gunshots came through, then, finally a reply.

"Espinoza here," the voice said. "Sent with a fire team by Colonel Walton. Where do you need us?"

"Perfect timing," Sandra replied. "There's a train station northwest of the city and some of our people are cut off there. Think you can make it over?"

"A rescue mission?" Espinoza paused, likely telling his team, then came back. "We see the spot and aren't too far off."

"Great. Valerie's there too and has a comm device, though she hasn't been answering. Maybe you can try when you get close."

"Roger that. She's probably in the thick of it, doesn't want to give away her position."

"I don't think she'd be too worried," Sandra replied, imagining Valerie tearing through her enemies. "But yes, her being too busy makes sense. Just…bring her back safe."

"We'll see you soon."

The comm device went to static and then turned off, leaving Sandra to stare at it for a moment. She almost wished she were out there kicking ass with them all. A child passed and looked up at her with a large smile, his eyes resting on her belly. She held it and said, "What's your name?"

"Kyle," he replied. "I'm ready to fight too. Just let me know."

She smiled, trying not to seem like she was mocking him. "Thank you, Kyle. How old are you?"

"Seven. But I've fought lots."

"We look forward to having you on our side then." She gave him an encouraging nod. "Stay vigilant."

He stood proudly and walked back to his parents.

Watching him and then joining the rest of them again, she smiled to herself. This was exactly where she belonged. She just hoped Espinoza and his team were getting close to Valerie and the others with her, and that the two groups didn't accidentally fire on each other.

CHAPTER TEN

Outside New York

For the tenth time, Valerie ignored the comm device as it signaled that someone was trying to get through. As much as she wanted to pick up and tell Sandra she and Diego were fine, she was a tad occupied.

The first move had been to get everyone out of the airship. Since making it straight to the city was unrealistic, she had led them all over to the old train station, setting them up in defensible hiding spots.

Although several small groups had run into the old railyard, they had been easy to take out. But now, as she watched the Pod open fire and zoom back toward them, she knew there was worse about to hit.

The first volley of grenades and rockets hit the airship, blasting it to smithereens. Good thing they'd cleared out of there, but it was only a matter of time before the attackers directed that same firepower at the train station.

On the one hand, it would be good to have them use up their explosives before the assault on New York. On the other, it could result in everyone's deaths.

"I'm moving up," she told Diego. "You can come with me or not. Micky, we need someone strong to stay back here and hold up the defense, keep these people safe."

"Count on me," Micky replied.

"And you know I'm going with you," Diego stated.

She nodded. "I figured. I'm going dark, so keep out of my way."

He laughed. "And you mine."

"Deal."

Garcia cleared his throat. "You two know I've got to cover your asses. I'll do my best to not cause trouble."

Valerie gave Diego a look that said she blamed him for this, but shrugged.

"If you three don't come back," Micky started as he moved his grip on his rifle, "how'll New York know we're on the right side when we show up at their doorstep?"

"If Lady Woo's forces are powerful enough to take us out," Valerie countered, "I wouldn't worry about making it to New York."

"Well, thanks for that," Micky grumbled.

"You want me to lie and pull rainbows out of my ass, or tell you how it is? Point of fact, you can't take on whatever they have that could actually kill us. Unless you have some magic you haven't told me about?"

Micky shook his head, not looking at her.

"That's what I thought. However, if all of this goes to hell but you somehow manage to make it to New York, just ask for Davies or Sandra and tell 'em I sent you. They'll treat you right."

She smiled in a way she hoped was encouraging and then, after pulling out her sword and her pistol, departed into the night. Diego's scent followed, though he couldn't keep up even when transformed. Somewhere back there Garcia was following too. She was pretty sure he could hold his own, but having a non-modified fighter out here amped up her worry level.

Running along old train tracks and ducking behind over-turned rusted rail cars, she had to wonder about the world before. A world where people used these and other modes of transportation to quickly move from city to city.

Had it led to more peace, or less? Judging by the fact that the people of that time had been the ones to bring about the Great Collapse, she doubted very much that it had been a good thing. Bringing people together made sense, but when technology reached levels where complete idiots had their hands on massive weapons that could bring the world to its knees, something was wrong.

A shot pinged off the door of a rail car she had passed moments ago and she knelt, eyes scanning the fallen boxcars and piles of garbage that occupied the grounds. Clouds were rolling in overhead, blocking out the moonlight. That meant she would have the advantage.

Giving a *push* of fear, she heard a quick gasp from ahead past a turned-over shipping crate. A moment later the man popped up, rifle blasting randomly. He was scared, shooting in hopes of making a lucky hit, and then—with a growl, as Diego pounced— he was dead.

Valerie darted forward, giving her friend a nod, and then aimed as two more shooters appeared. They were dead before they processed her arrival.

To their right the airship was still in flames, casting deep shadows behind the surrounding shipping containers and rail cars. Smoke billowed over the railyard, so much now that its scent was blocking Valerie's keen sense of smell.

While losing olfactory and visual perception was annoying, she could still sense emotions of those nearby, which would help her locate anyone she couldn't see or smell. Judging by the look of frustration on Diego's cat-face when he came up behind her, he was more frustrated by the smoke issue.

"Get to the far side and we'll start picking them off before they realize where the others are," Valerie whispered, then pointed to the place she was talking about.

With a nod Diego moved out, his legs tense and ready to pounce should trouble present itself.

Valerie followed, but then moved in an arc so she could approach from a different tangent.

Her comm device vibrated, and she shook her head. Sword held out behind her, pistol up and at the ready, she charged forward. The men and women who had blasted the airship to bits were advancing in a line, weapons moving from right to left as they passed railcar after railcar looking for their prey.

Valerie enjoyed lines. It was like they were all waiting for her to cut through them. As if they were begging for it.

A man passed a shipping container and vanished, followed by a quick yelp.

"Over here!" one of the men shouted, and the four closest followed suit. They leaped forward and fired, only to stop and stare in confusion. Then a growl sounded from behind them and Diego was pouncing again, taking them out.

Valerie watched some of this and decided it was her turn. Eyes glowing red and feeling energy surge through her and pump her up, she ran for them, pistol blasting the first three before she was close enough to use her sword. That was when the slaughter began.

Like a child kicking off the heads off dandelions, she ran through them, sword slashing and blood splattering. Heads fell, bowels were emptied, and guts spewed forth as more and more of them collapsed.

When she had gone through half the line the others realized what was happening and broke, diving for cover. Screams followed as Diego tore into one and then another while shots were fired in Valerie's direction.

She dove to the side behind an old door hanging half off its hinges. Bullets pinged off it, giving her an idea. She leaped up and pulled the door free and then, holding the door by its handle, used it like a shield as she charged. She thrust it out and the door hit one man, sending him flying into an overturned locomotive's wheels behind him. She moved on as a barrage of automatic rifles spat at her.

Some of the metal of the door had been chipped away and several bullets went right through, grazing her mostly, but one hit her in the gut.

Pain. Horrible pain. *She didn't like pain.*

With a shout of anger, she *pushed* fear and threw the door at them. Half of them fell back in confusion and fright as the door took one in the head. By the time any of them processed what was happening she was on them, cutting them down as the hole in her belly healed.

A quick worried growl came from Diego and Valerie turned in time to see a flamethrower being used nearby. While she was pretty damn powerful, she didn't know if her body could heal fast enough to be okay with damage from a flamethrower.

More shots accompanied it and she saw a flood of new fighters surging into the grounds.

Then shots came from behind and some started to fall. She leaped out of the way of the flames, pulling her pistol.

Again the comm device vibrated and she was about to hurl it at her opponents, but instead she picked it up in her moment of frustration and answered.

"I'm a bit fucking busy!" she shouted into it, instantly regretting talking to Sandra like that.

But it wasn't Sandra's voice that came through.

"Someone called for an extermination crew?" a male voice said, chuckling. "You just sit back and keep on killing them from your end. We'll do our thing over here."

"Who is this?" she said between shots, the most recent one hitting the flamethrower's pack, which exploded and took out several nearby.

"Nice shot!" he said.

She spun, searching, and saw more shooting in both directions farther off.

"Name's Espinoza," the voice said. "Colonel Walton sent us."

"Terry-Henry Walton?"

"The same."

Valerie smiled, squinting to see if she could make them out in the distance. "Well, why didn't you say so? Stop goofing off over there and come help me kill these assholes."

He laughed. "We're working on it. Any chance you can clear a path and meet us in the middle?"

"I'll see you in five," she replied.

"Five minutes won't be—"

"Five seconds." She darted out with a new level of excitement and shouted for Diego to try and keep up.

A whimper sounded in response, but he came.

Each second was marked by a slash of her sword, the swipe of her claws, and strikes that stole her enemies' lives without mercy.

"Four one-thousand," she counted, driving the sword through a man's body so hard that the force tore him in two. "Five one-thousand." She spun, sword out, but stopped with the tip inches from a man's throat.

"That was precise," he said, grimacing at the sword. "Do you mind?"

"Confirmation?"

"It's me—Espinoza—sent by Colonel Walton." Shots went off around them as his team, anxiously glancing at her, held their position.

She lowered the sword and extended a hand, which he accepted. "Good, now let's get these people out of here."

"This is it?" he asked, glancing over her shoulder at Diego.

"They're back there, by the—" Shots from the train station interrupted her. "Shit! Stay on my tail!"

Anyone else would've made a joke right then, considering

Diego's rapid transformation and the fact that Colonel Walton was known to be romantically involved with a Were, but Espinoza just checked his rifle and signaled his men to follow. *A testament to his military professionalism*, she thought, *though perhaps a tad boring*.

Valerie returned just in time to intercept a group of four men, two preparing a rocket launcher while another loaded a rifle. The man watching their backs had enough time to yelp at the sight of Valerie with her glowing red eyes before his head left his body. The others turned in shock, one pissing himself, while Valerie threw the man with the grenade back toward his own forces. Diego tore into the man with the rocket launcher, which he snatched out of the air before it fell.

A glance backward showed a line of shooters, giving her an idea where the majority of the group was. Many were still advancing on New York.

This could be fun, she thought as she prepared the rocket launcher. She had used one in training long ago under her brother's supervision, but never like this, and never against people who actually deserved to die.

With a blast of power it was off, the rocket screaming through the air, and then it hit and she wanted to laugh like a child at Christmas. Too bad she had friends to help right now.

She turned to see a man running at her and hefted the rocket launcher like a baseball bat. *BAM!* His head went flying right back into the smoldering flames where the rocket had exploded.

"Damn, no wonder the Colonel wants you to live through this," Espinoza said with a whistle as he witnessed this. "I heard he's starting a softball league."

"Oh, so the soldier actually *does* have a sense of humor."

He laughed. "When I see shit like that I'm torn between vomiting all over myself or making a joke. Guess which one I pick?"

"Fair enough." She dropped the rocket launcher and drew her sword again.

They kept moving toward the train station, now behind the enemy. But as Espinoza's team started picking them off, Valerie noticed a group moving toward the side of the building, otherwise unnoticed.

"I'll be right back," she hissed in case anyone could hear her as she darted after them. Screams came from behind as Diego tore into more of the enemy, and shots flew all around.

None of it fazed Valerie, though. She was in the zone. With so much fighting lately, this had become the new normal for her.

"Hey, jackasses!" she shouted as she plowed through the group, taking the lead man with her. She leaped up onto a train with him before breaking him over her knee and dropping his squirming form to the ground for effect. "The last of you to be holding a gun dies the most painful death. If you surrender, I've been known to let defectors switch to our side. Your choice. Ten seconds."

To her surprise, one man dropped his rifle and stepped back. Unfortunately, the woman to his right lifted her pistol and shot him in the head before turning the weapon on Valerie.

Or, at least, where Valerie had been a moment ago—now she was on the ground, sprinting to the woman's side and driving her sword through the woman's arm. She twisted and it popped off, leaving the woman to back away screaming.

"Time's almost up," Valerie stated, stepping forward as she drove the sword into the woman's foot, pinning her in place. "But I've changed my mind. This woman dies slowest. The rest of you? Let's find out."

Five of them were left, two taking a step back and looking unsure, a third turning and making a run for it.

That left two courageous idiots to try and kill her. She shook her head, let down. She had hoped they would be smart enough to all surrender or all attack at once—none of this half-assed teamwork.

Oh well, they were probably the type she wouldn't want on her side anyway, if that was their level of discipline.

Since it sounded like the others had the assault under control, she decided to freshen up on her hand-to-hand combat. When the first man came at her swinging his rifle like he was going to butt-stroke her, she leaped aside like a lion pouncing, following the motion with a kick to the man's leg that sent him to his knees. A one-two punch combo sent him to the ground, dead.

The other wasn't as much fun, running at her and screaming. All it took was a punch to the throat and it was over. Since one of her punches could obliterate a wall, it wasn't surprising that it brought such carnage to a soft throat, but still, she had been looking forward to a fight.

Judging by the sound of gunfire out there and the numbers she had seen, she would have her chance. Right now it was time to reconnect with Espinoza and the team and get everyone to safety.

Diego and Garcia had already met up with Cammie, Royland, and the others and just taken out the last of their attackers when a new round of shots sounded from the east side of the building.

He paused, then held a hand up to stop Garcia from firing down the platform.

"I think we're good."

Garcia frowned. "Maybe your Were ears aren't as good as I thought."

"We have reinforcements."

"Oh?"

A final shot and then forms appeared, emerging from the

platform exit. "Garcia, you old bull, the balls you've got coming out here without us!"

Garcia frowned, then his eyes lit up. "No shit! Is that you, Espinoza?"

A second later the two groups were running at each other. Garcia had embraced each of them in turn and was introducing them to Micky and the others.

"These ol' bastards served with me under Colonel Walton," he explained. "Espinoza here's one of the hardest men around, and I don't just mean in the bedroom."

"The hell do you know about me in the bedroom?" Espinoza said, mock-punching him in the gut. "Your mom been telling stories again?"

"Oh, hell no." Garcia held out his rifle. "Someone take this before I shoot one of my best buddies."

"Boys," came another welcome voice—Valerie's, "do try to act like gentlemen when ladies are present."

"Hey, our ladies can dish it out as good as either of those two," Micky countered, giving a nod to the redhead beside him. "Probably take 'em in a fight, too."

"I was talking about me," she replied with a grin. "And I *know* I could take them both, so let's not start pissing in the wind and hoping it doesn't come back to haunt us. Everyone ready?"

"My apologies," Espinoza stated.

Espinoza and Garcia returned to their alert, battle-ready stances, the others moving to the areas where walls had once stood, weapons at the ready in case there was trouble. Cammie was at the edge of one of the broken walls, Royland at the other, using their keen sight as lookouts.

Garcia spared another glance at his friend.

"If the Colonel knew you'd gotten so relaxed in your old age he'd have your *cajones* in a jar, *cabrón*."

"Fuck that," Espinoza countered. "I'm about to ensure every one of you makes it back to New York without a scratch on you."

Valerie smirked. "Good. I'd like to hear your plan."

"Some of us don't gotta worry about getting scratched," Cammie commented from her vantage point. "Worry about your own hide."

The man gave her a middle finger, but pulled it back at a look from Royland.

"So?" Valerie asked.

He motioned to the building. "This place used to connect to the city, right? I mean, it's a train station with a subway connection, I'd think. Gotta be a way in underground."

Valerie glanced at the group. "We'd be sitting ducks in there if they found us and made a move."

Espinoza raised an eyebrow. "With you and your eyes? I doubt there'd be a chance of them catching us unawares."

"What about the fact that the subways were blocked off over the years?" Diego interjected. "I mean, there's bound to be a barrier in the way at some point."

"Then we fucking move it," Cammie interjected.

Diego laughed, then saw that she was serious. He shrugged.

"It's settled then," Valerie said. "It does make sense, actually. If we tried to make a move aboveground with a group like ours, we'd be bound to at least take a stray bullet."

"A stray bullet or a thousand," Arturo said, stepping up next to Micky. "I got a look at what's out there. They've got a mighty big force, and they're moving in to surround us."

"You got any explosives on you?" Valerie asked Espinoza.

He nodded. "Not enough, but...oh, to blow the entrance to the subway?"

She nodded.

"We'd be trapped in there," Diego countered. "If there isn't another way out, we'd be sealing our own tomb."

"You're against the idea?" she asked. "Should we let them follow us down there?"

He scrunched his nose in thought, then shook his head. "No way."

"Exactly." She turned to Espinoza and nodded. "Let's find this subway entrance and get the hell out of here."

"Already found it," Arturo noted, nodding to his left. "Problem is, the south side of their forces is blocking it. We'll need a diversion."

Valerie smiled. "Count on me. When I give the signal, it's go-time."

"And the signal will be?" Diego asked.

"A bunch of screaming from their side, followed by death." With that she sprinted out of there, heading southwest, the direction Arturo had pointed her in.

"Well, that's the plan then," Diego said. "Everyone, get ready to move."

"Everyone," Espinoza said, turning to his men. "Get ready to move."

"I just…said that."

Espinoza smiled at Diego with a shrug. "My men, my orders."

"You military types…" Diego just shook his head and went to check on Micky and the others, who had already started moving over to the far wall, preparing to evacuate.

"Everyone holding up?" he asked when he and Micky had settled down, looking outward and preparing for the signal.

"Me and mine, we're used to this shit," Micky replied. "The Badlands would be called the Goodlands if they were filled with pots of gold and rainbows. You know?"

"Cut the shit, Micky."

Micky grinned, his large face transforming him from an intimidating ogre of a man to a friendly teddy bear with such a simple act.

"You aren't wrong," Cammie told Micky. "Sooner I can get out of here and never have to go into the Badlands again, the sooner I'll be smiling for life."

"Micky, your people," Diego repeated. "How are they doing?"

"Hell, man. They're doing fine, but the moment this is all behind us, I'll be a happy camper. If there's a real possibility for peace in this world? A city life with city comforts behind the walls of New York? Color me purple and call me Jane, because I'll be mind-blown."

Diego laughed. "It's a deal, Jane."

"Hey, none of that. You haven't proven shit to me yet."

"Tell you what, when we get in there we're going to go straight to my wife's place. She has a café, if you want to call it that. Wine, croissants... Oh, did I mention she came over from Old France? Yeah, woman knows her cheeses too."

Micky pursed his lips, then nodded. "You're selling me on this, and I'm buying. Maybe I'll pick up myself one of those wife-women things while I'm at it."

"Women things?" Diego chuckled. "Man, you talk like that in New York and some *woman thing* is going to bust your lip open. Shit, you do so around Valerie or my wife, you'll be hanging from the tallest building by your balls. Just saying."

"This some sort of Amazon-controlled woman rulership place? I didn't sign up for that."

"No, man. What I'm saying is it's equal there. I don't know how it is in the Badlands or back in El Diablo, but in New York, hell, most of the new world pretty soon I'd say, you gotta watch how you talk about women, and they gotta watch how they talk about us. Some *chica* says she's going to get some meat sticks, I'm going to be offended just like these women would be offended if you say you're going to a taco buffet. That's what I mean."

Micky tried not to laugh at that, but a small one escaped. "I get it, I get it. But the whole...tallest building thing?"

"An exaggeration...I hope. I've never tested it, and wouldn't want to."

"You and me both, my man." Micky held out his hand for a fist bump, but Diego, unsure what to do there, shook it, earning him another laugh.

"The two of you're having a damn good time," Garcia said, walking over, "considering we're about to run out into a possible barrage of bullets."

"I'm not worried," Diego replied with a shrug. "Val says she's on it, she's on it."

Garcia nodded. "That chick—"

"That woman," Micky said, correcting him and then turning to Diego, beaming and waiting for a nod of approval, which Diego gave.

"Right..." Garcia looked confused, but continued, "That woman is badass. Her and TH, I mean the Colonel, if they ever fight side-by-side? Fucking hold on to your socks, boys. I mean it —anyone tries to stand up to those two when they're on the same side? Green eggs and ham."

"I... I'm sorry," Diego said, liking everything he'd just heard but being totally lost by the food reference.

"Oh, just something I say." Garcia shrugged. "You know, enemy brains smeared on the wall like eggs, and... Oh, hell, I don't know. I had this half a book cover growing up, put it on my wall like a poster. All it said was "Green Eggs and Ham," so I kinda started saying that whenever I referred to someone getting the shit blasted out of them."

"Weird, but that's about the norm around here," Diego said with a chuckle, and the other two laughed.

"I'll second that," Cammie said, "and serve as an example."

Their laughter was cut short as a shot sounded, followed by screams in the night, another barrage of shots, an explosion, and then more screams.

It sent a chill down Diego's spine along with instant images of his wife and child alone, without him, staring at his grave. Well, there wasn't any way in hell he was going to let that happen, so he pushed his fear aside and stood.

"Come on, you sons of bitches, do you want to sit here waiting forever?!"

"Hell no!" Garcia said through gritted teeth, and he and Micky stood with Diego, the rest of them following close behind as they led the charge out of there.

Valerie was one with the shadow, diving behind old ruins and leaping out to break a neck, then sinking into the trench behind the men only to come up a moment later and tear into them with claws and teeth. She left the sword out of it this time so moonlight glinting on steel wouldn't give her away. It wasn't warrior time right now—it was horror time.

If ever there had been vampires like the stories of old, demons of the night, at this moment she was the embodiment of that evil. But she was on the side of the righteous, here to send fear into the hearts of those who would otherwise harm the innocent of New York.

A general aura of fear was now permeating the men and women there, who had scattered and were shooting randomly as they tried to find her between kills. It was like a fog that only she could see, one that didn't obscure her vision but told her she was being successful.

From behind, where she had left her team, another type of emotion was strong—courage. She sensed it like a warm breeze on an otherwise cool night. She glanced back to see them on the move, small shapes keeping low as they ran to avoid being noticed.

The plan was working.

With a roar she came up on her prey, eyes glowing bright red in the night, and took one of them with her as she leaped into the air. Her goal was to make it appear as if she had flown, biting into him as they reached the peak of her jump and then dropping the body amongst his comrades.

The effect was instantaneous. Fighters scattered to the wind, not even bothering to try and shoot anymore.

All but a small group of them, now alone in the open—maybe twenty. Judging by their scent, the group was a mixture of Weres and Forsaken.

That didn't worry her. What worried her was that now that the group had dispersed they had noticed her friends making a move for the subway behind her. The Weres and Forsaken split into several group of two to three and were working to get around Valerie.

"Fight *me*!" she shouted, charging the ones closest to her friends. They had no interest in her, though, at least not until she reached that trio and tore into one of the Weres even as he transformed, ripping his wolf head from his body and tossing it at one of the vampires.

That vampire stumbled over the head, but tossed it aside and kept running.

At this speed the groups were closing in on her friends. Garcia and Micky, with a couple others, were shooting back, and Diego had transformed, moving out to meet the attack.

Instead of trying to stop the enemy, she changed direction and went straight for Diego and the others so that she could stand with them in defense. The more of these bastards she could face at once, the better chance she had of killing them in large numbers.

"Get in there and blow the explosives!" she shouted to Garcia.

She spotted Espinoza, whose team was mostly prone, aiming at a trio and filling them full of holes.

"Not without you!" Espinoza shouted, rolling over to grab another magazine. "I'm running low!" he called and someone next to him tossed over another mag.

With a growl two Weres leaped for Valerie, teeth dangerously close to sinking into her. She spun, kicked one off, and came up with her sword drawn. She charged the closest and sliced it in two, then thrust the blade through the skull of the second.

"Do it now!" Valerie shouted. "That's a fucking order!"

Garcia knew enough about Valerie to understand that when she swore—which wasn't often—she meant business. He was already up and pulled Espinoza with him. The rest of the team followed.

"Go!" Valerie told Diego too, swinging for a vampire. He dodged and went for Garcia, but she pierced his leg and made him stumble back where Garcia finished him off. She shooed him away. "I'll be right behind you!"

He hesitated, but then Cammie came charging through with Royland, tearing through more of the enemy as they cleared the route. Garcia turned to join the others as they disappeared down an old overgrown staircase.

Now all she had to do was defend the entrance instead of worrying about people getting shot.

A duo came from her left while a trio tried to get around her to make it to the staircase, but then she was among them, spinning and thrusting and slicing. This group had their own blades and they connected plenty of times, but never enough to cause her to pause or worry.

Limbs and heads flew and then another Were was on her, snarling as saliva dripped down his teeth. He knocked her over, snapping at her face.

"Gross," she muttered between gritted teeth, then bit off his nasty moist nose and spat it out. As the wolf howled, she snatched out his larynx and tossed it aside.

Her hand went for her sword, but she had dropped it. When she reached for it, her blood-drenched hand couldn't quite grip it. Grunting in frustration, she tore off part of her shirt and wrapped it around her hand, then reached for the sword again.

Another vampire hit her, driving his knife into her side and likely striking a kidney.

She growled, more out of anger than pain, and hit him with an elbow before turning to slice his face off, followed by two quick hacks at the neck.

"Get down here, Val!" Cammie shouted.

Instead she turned to take on another attacker, quickly bashing the female vampire's head in with the pommel of her sword.

"Dammit," now it was Royland, "get down here now or I'm coming back up to drag you down myself!"

Valerie hesitated now, considering. She knew none of them had the strength to overcome her, but she didn't want any of them at risk—especially Diego. Sandra would eat her alive if she let Diego get hurt.

Without another thought she leaped backward, taking all the stairs at once, and shouted, *"Blow it!"*

Others cleared out and then there was Espinoza smiling like a boy about to let off a firework, and...

KA-BOOM!

They were all thrown down into the darkness along with a blast of debris as the explosion closed the entrance above. Only, as Valerie glanced around, she saw forms moving closer to the explosion, one of them putting out a small fire on its arm.

When they looked at her, she saw red eyes.

"Go!" she shouted to her friends. "Some of them made it down. *Go!*"

As she stood to fight, the vampires moved into side tunnels and passageways, splitting directions. She could take on the best, but she couldn't be in more than one place at a time. Instead of trying to go after them, she moved back to Garcia.

"Keep the group together," she commanded. "If you see movement, tell me."

Moving as one, everyone staying close with eyes searching the darkness in all directions and guns at the ready, they moved down the tunnel that had once been allowed commuters to reach Manhattan.

While Royland and Cammie served as point, they were also leading them in the extreme darkness. As long as they could hear him moving, they were good.

They were being hunted, and it pissed Valerie off.

But for the time being at least, there wasn't much she could do about it.

CHAPTER ELEVEN

New York

Sandra was helping Clara go over the hand-to-hand combat techniques she had learned in her time with the Forsaken in Old France. Clara had been a pirate and knew how to shoot and the basics of fighting, particularly when it came to keep someone off her, but she hadn't ever been properly trained.

Not many of these people had, Sandra realized after a glance around her. They were watching, some starting to practice the blocks and counter-strikes on their own.

Well, that wouldn't do.

"Everyone find a partner and try to imitate me," Sandra said, and then waited for them to partner up.

"I promise," Clara said while they waited, using the moment to stretch, "that if we ever have to use this, I'll fight your attacker off before anyone else's."

Sandra nodded. "Normally I'd say I don't need it, but yeah... Given the circumstances, I might take you up on that."

The others were ready, so she had Clara come at her as if holding a knife, then demonstrated a simple move to disarm her. She stepped sideways and hit the arm with her left forearm, then grabbed and bent the arm in using her other hand so that the knife turned in on her opponent.

When she was done she had others try, and walked around giving pointers. "This might not help you if the fight comes today," Sandra told them, "but if you keep practicing and someone comes at you tomorrow, the next day, or a week from now, who knows?"

"You really think this will go on for that long?" a boy asked.

She shook her head. "Once vampires and Weres are in the mix, no. These things tend to go a lot faster than they would otherwise when that happens."

The room looked uneasy at that, so Sandra decided she had better be upfront about everything.

"Keep practicing," she said, walking among the with her hands behind her back. "The fact is, vampires and Weres aren't all bad. They are definitely not what you've heard about in your bedtime stories or whatever version you might have been told. They are simply modified humans. In fact, my husband is a Were."

"Like he turns into a wolf?"

She laughed. "More like a cute little cat, but don't tell him I said so." That got her some chuckles, which helped the room relax. "The point is that you shouldn't ever be scared about something just because of your preconceived notions. Fire kills. It burns. But it also cooks food and gives us light. You see?"

A couple of them nodded, and Sandra noticed the Were son in the back smiling her way. She hadn't even thought about how he must feel in here, and had noticed him following her around a bit. Now she got it, as she smiled back. Down here she was one of the very few who knew what he was—who got him—to the extent that anyone could understand someone who's a Were when you yourself weren't.

She was considering going over to him when a commotion sounded in the hall. At first she took a defensive stance, considering their options, getaway routes, and fastest way to the weapons, but then she recognized the voice. Jackson.

He came around the corner with three large men following.

"They're coming this way, more of them," Jackson said. "Whatever happened out there, they've stopped shooting and fighting and the enemy is moving toward our walls."

Sandra turned and looked at all the scared faces. She could tell them all to go away so they wouldn't have to hear this... But no, it was their war too, their city.

"Val, the others..." She ran a hand through her hair. "They couldn't have lost. Right?"

"That's what I'm going to find out," he replied. "I've got a team, even that werebear. We're going to fly north, lights off, then cut across. It might take us some time to get out there and around, but it'll be safer than going straight through that horde. We just wanted to let you know because—"

"Because Diego is out there. Yeah, I get it."

"And because... You have the comm device, right?"

She wanted to punch herself. There hadn't been any answer the last few times she had tried, so she had kind of given up. Now she was terrified, though. If they didn't pick up this time she would have to assume the worst.

Hand shaking, she went to her bag, which she had tossed in the corner, pulled out the device, and buzzed Valerie.

The rest of the room was silent, some leaving out of apparent pity or whatever. And it continued to signal, not connecting. When she finally gave up, she sat there staring at it. They weren't fighting, so why no answer?

"It doesn't mean anything," Jackson promised. "We're going to the crash site. We'll get the answers."

Sandra nodded slowly, trying to think of what to say. Her hand went to her belly and she imagined a world where Diego never came back. *Fuck!* She'd never been the type to need someone else, but in this she desperately wanted him there. Her child *needed* its dad.

"I'm coming too," she said.

"Like hell you are," Jackson replied, staring at her aghast. "You think I'm taking a pregnant woman into that, you're fucking nuts."

"I *am* fucking nuts, and my husband, the father of my soon-to-be-born child, is possibly hurt out there. Who knows? I'm not going to sit here wondering!"

Jackson had opened his mouth to argue further when the comm device buzzed.

"Holy shit," Sandra said, nearly dropping it as she turned it to the see the screen. The hope that had burst forth was just as fast killed as she saw the name. *Espinoza*. For all she knew—in fact she was suddenly sure of it—the person was calling to tell her they had found Diego's body.

She just stared.

"Answer it already!" Jackson snapped, voice breaking. He took it and said, "This is Jackson, here with Sandra. What's going on?"

"The other device," Espinoza replied. "It's not working down here for some reason. But the call showed up momentarily, so here..."

"Sandra?" Diego's voice came in. "Are you there? Is everything oka—"

"Diego? Don't you dare not answer when I'm calling, do you understand?"

"Dear, the comm device, it—"

"I don't care if you have to jump into the sky and yell as loud as you can or tie a note to a pigeon's leg—whatever. I don't care. Just answer!"

There was long pause, and a couple laughs could be heard in the background before Diego said, "Yes, I understand. Of course, dear."

Jackson leaned in gingerly, as if scared she might bite him. "Diego, where are you all? The forces are moving for our walls."

"So are we, just…underground."

"What?" Sandra asked, glancing around as if he might walk through the walls at any moment.

"Yes, through the subway. But it might be blocked off ahead, and…we're not alone down here. See if you can figure out the route this would have taken, then start clearing the way from your side. Have some defenses set up in case there are problems. We'll—"

Suddenly he stopped talking, but someone was whispering about seeing movement.

"Just do it," Diego whispered. "Gotta go. Sandra, I love you."

"I love you too."

The other side disconnected and Sandra bit her lip. A thought hit her. "The old subway map! When we were down here that first time just after saving the vampires from the blood banks, yeah."

She took off running, Jackson and his men following.

Soon they were at the old map. It was falling to pieces, torn behind glass that was mostly intact, but not all the way. Still, they could see approximately where the train would have come in from.

"I know that tunnel," Jackson said. When Sandra gave him a confused look, he continued, "You know I led my people. Sometimes that meant being in the subways. Hiding out, planning a move, whatever the reasons, does it matter now?"

"No," she said, beaming as hope flooded her body again. "Let's get to it, then."

He looked her over, doubtful for a moment, but nodded. "Right, of course. Come on!"

CHAPTER TWELVE

Subway Tunnels

Moving through the tunnels wasn't pleasant, not knowing when the vampires that had come down might strike. Valerie could smell them from time to time, but they were relocating too fast to pinpoint them.

At least they had gotten through to Sandra so Diego could be at ease, and vice versa.

Cammie and Royland continued to be dual point at the front in case any attackers tried to block the group's forward movement. Valerie, for her part, had decided to hang back a bit, seeing if she could bait any of the vampires into trying to take her on their own.

It worked.

A growl sounded as two of them came at her, one with two short blades, the other just with his claws.

She glanced over her shoulder to make sure the group was out of range of being in trouble from these two at least. As long as she moved fast.

The blades came at her and she ducked over the ledge that led to tracks below, long ago covered with debris. As he followed she met him with her sword, so that he fell without one of his legs. The other one was smarter, jumping to the side and hissing, but she charged and impaled him, pinning him to a piece of rotten wood before ripping him to shreds with her claws.

A shot came from the group and she saw another vampire moving in the dark, so she gave chase. She used the one-legged vampire as a stepstool, being sure to jam her sword through his head as she did so.

Once back up on the platform, she ran to the other corridor where she'd seen him go, then froze, relying on her other senses. He wasn't in sight, but there was a distinct odor like mold and onions to her left.

She caught a movement and braced herself, then nearly shat as she saw Royland dart around the bend. He was ready for a fight, but when he saw her alone he paused, eyes searching the darkness.

"Get back with the group," she commanded.

"I won't let you face them alone," he replied.

"And if they come for Cammie? Maybe two on one? I can handle that, but while she's tough…I'm not sure."

He hesitated, snarled, and then turned back to do as she'd ordered.

No more shots came, only the sound of a couple commands from Garcia along with the shuffles and clangs of movement. Why couldn't they be quieter? It was hard to remember the clumsiness of nonmodified humans when you had the grace of a vampire.

Sinking into the shadows, she moved along the edge of the corridor and found a doorway. Within was an old maintenance shed—apparently empty, but her sense of smell told her otherwise. It gave her just enough warning to jump back as a vampire appeared from a hole in the ceiling she might not have otherwise noticed.

He tried to spear her with a long metal rod, bent and sharp.

This one was fast and moved as if trained. She couldn't move well in this area, not with the sword, so she backed up—but not far enough, she learned when the point of the spear sliced across her shirt. Too close!

Pissed now, she waited for the next strike and this time let it come. She moved into the spear, just off to the side, and swatted it so hard that it hit the wall beside her and sent a shock up the holder's arm. It was strong enough to cause him to drop the rod, stumbling back as she first landed an elbow in his face and then slammed her knuckles into his throat.

Vampires didn't die so easily, however, so she finished him off with his own weapon.

"*Val!*" Garcia shouted, and then she heard shots and clangs of metal.

No rest for kickass heroines, huh? She sighed, took a deep breath, and ran, reaching them to see Royland darting across the other side in a chase while a female vampire dragged someone off. Valerie pursued her and caught the dragger at the last minute, but not before the female vampire had sunk her teeth into the man in her grasp. It was a large man in a leather jacket, and for a moment Valerie thought it was Micky. She hated the relief she felt when she noticed long blond dreadlocks. No Micky at all in the look of death staring back at her.

As the vampire turned on her, she realized why the man was dead. Blood covered her front from mouth to torso. She must've gotten to the man before this bite.

"You're not mine to kill," Valerie stated, then dug her fingernails into the eyes of the vampire and popped them out before grabbing her head and slamming it into the ground.

In a dazed, pained shouting fit of rage and confusion, the vampire struggled as Valerie dragged her back to Micky and Arturo.

"I assume you want to deal with this piece of rotten shit?"

Arturo stepped forward, Micky giving him room.

"This is for my brother, you rat fart-eating shit stain-licking piece of fuckstick!" He stomped on the vampire's head repeatedly while Garcia worked to keep the rest of the group moving, especially Fred and Eddie Jr.

"Fuck 'em," Micky said, spitting on the limp vampire when Arturo was done and the vampire lay still. He handed over a knife and Arturo finished her off.

"I'm sorry," Valerie said, senses still on high alert but taking a moment to be there for them. "I didn't know you had a brother."

Arturo gave her a nod of appreciation and returned to the group, shouting along the way, "Any of you other sons of bitches wants some, come on! I'm right here!"

Just then, Royland came stumbling back, a cut slowly healing across his cheek, but otherwise good. He frowned at the sight and said, "Got the other one."

Cammie took up the spot at his side again and they moved to the front of the group to continue down the tunnel.

Micky checked his gun, glancing back, and Valerie now decided to stick with the group. She had taken enough of the vampires out that she doubted they had much of a numerical advantage on her anymore.

Royland and Cammie led the charge as the snarling of fighting vampires grew closer behind them. Valerie could easily take them, but here, moving about as they were—in and out like assassins in the night—he didn't have as much confidence. It wasn't her; it was the ability of the others to move at the same time from different angles.

It didn't matter who you were—nobody could be more than one place at a time.

"There!" Garcia pointed, turning down the main corridor and

running along the tracks. It had to be the way out. The main track that led into the city.

But as they turned, they came to the sight they all had known would come, though all had hoped it wouldn't.

There was a wall of chunks of cement and scrap metal, likely put up at some point to keep outsiders from sneaking into the city. It was working in a sense, but at the worst possible time.

"Get the path cleared!" Royland shouted, already starting to fling rocks out of the way as Cammie joined him.

Others moved in too while Espinoza and his team formed a line, rifles at the ready.

"There won't be time," Micky shouted from Garcia's side as the two helped. He was moving what looked like a large metal wheel out of the way.

"There are only so many of them," Garcia replied. "Eventually Val will find them all. By then we'll be through."

"Let's hope so," he replied.

A shot went off, then several more, and Garcia turned to see a vampire fall from the ceiling. Two more came at them and then suddenly Valerie was there, leaping from the wall to grab one and pull it to the floor. She commenced beating it to death while others shot at the one above. It dropped, though, right onto Valerie, and she had to roll aside to get it off.

She moved with precision, quickly drawing her sword and removing the vampire's head. Without a moment's hesitation, she disappeared again into the darkness to hunt more of them.

"Keep them going!" Micky shouted to a couple of people who had turned to watch, but just then Espinoza and the others started firing into the darkness. The shadow they were shooting at dodged left and right, avoiding the shots and coming closer.

"I'm going after them," Royland growled, turning to prepare for a fight.

"We all are," Garcia agreed, unslinging his rifle. "This isn't getting us anywhere.

Bullets weren't doing a damn thing. Preparing for the worst, Garcia took a stance next to Diego as he transformed, then nodded.

Royland and Cammie shared a look that said they were ready for whatever lay ahead, whether it meant victory or that it was their time to move on.

As the group was about to charge forward, however, voices sounded from behind them and then someone yelled, "*CLEAR!*" followed by a click and then...

KA-BOOM!

The wall behind them crumbled, parts of it flying out and raining down debris. When he looked back, it was clear. Sandra and Jackson were looking through and several of their fighters charged, including a bear that went straight for the oncoming vampire.

"*Fuck yeah!*" Garcia shouted, motioning the rest of their group back. "Get in there! We'll cover you!"

He opened fire and Diego ran forward. The shooters had to stop as the Weres and Royland met the enemy vampire, and soon they had had him overwhelmed.

Valerie ran up as the bear tore the vampire's head off with its jaws, and Diego transformed back.

"Any more?" Garcia asked, running up next to her.

"If there are," she replied, taking a moment to sniff the air, "I can't sense them. That *should* mean no, but just in case, get everyone out of here and let's close this tunnel back up."

"Roger that," he replied, and saw to it. He couldn't help laughing at the way Diego and Sandra were arguing right there in front of everyone, but had to agree with Diego. It wasn't safe for her to have come.

"Just thank her for rescuing you already and get over it," he said as he moved past the two, ducking through the semi-cleared passage. Royland and Cammie were right behind him.

Diego glared, but then, with a shrug to acknowledge he was right, hauled Sandra in for a kiss.

"Save it for outside the vampire trap," Valerie shouted with a laugh. "*Damn.*"

After they were on the other side of the wall Espinoza stayed to block up the passage with a couple of his guys, so Garcia did too.

Valerie lingered a moment to watch with a few of the other warriors as Sandra and Diego led most of them back to the underground hideouts.

"We'll have to go back out there," Valerie noted.

"Shit," Espinoza said as they moved back from the walls and set up another charge. "If the Colonel had known the extent of what was happening here, he would've sent more soldiers."

"He doesn't have so many to begin with, does he?" Garcia asked.

Espinoza shrugged. "All I'm saying is, we've got our work cut out for us."

"Don't forget, New York has fighters," Valerie replied. "We aren't going to just lay down our arms and surrender."

"Good." Espinoza nodded and an explosion followed, sending rocks from the ceiling down to block up the hole again.

"We'll need more shooters on the wall," Valerie went on, "and something tells me your guys can hit their marks."

"Damn straight," one of his guys said, a tall one with a hooked nose and olive skin.

"Best in the land," another agreed, checking his ears after the explosion.

Royland raised a finger and said, "Cammie and I, maybe we should defend the city."

Valerie nodded.

"I'll want Garcia and Micky," Valerie said. "We'll use several Pods to carry others who want to fight, but I'll need Espinoza and his men on the walls. People who can really shoot. My Weres and vampires are damn good fighters, but none of them are trained like they are. Plus, that's all the Pod can fit, considering Fred will need a lift."

"Speaking of Pods," Espinoza said, glaring at the new wall he had just made. "I'll need to recover ours at some point."

"We left one too," Garcia noted, then he frowned in thought. "You're sending Fred back out there? After the shit we just went through?"

"He's our best shot at turning some of them to our side. I shouldn't have to remind anyone here that we want to take as few lives as possible."

"Roger that," Espinoza replied.

"So when are we heading out?" Garcia asked.

She thought about it, then turned and started walking. "Immediately."

All of them got through the tunnels, glad to be back in the city. But as soon as Garcia made his way above ground he froze, turned to Valerie behind him, and said, "Looks like we have company."

She frowned, turned to follow his line of sight, and said, "What the hell?"

Moving toward them, having already passed the city walls and much of Central Park, were three airships. To his surprise, when she turned back to face him she was smiling.

"Not company," she said, "help. Get back to HQ and make sure everyone knows not to fire on those ships."

"Roger that," he said and took off, wondering what kind of help might have just arrived.

"Garcia, wait!"

"Yes, boss?"

She smiled. "I'm coming too."

CHAPTER THIRTEEN

North of New York

The look on her dad's face made Robin cringe almost as much as seeing the army marching on New York. She hadn't brought her family and the others from Toronto down here for war. In fact, she had thought bringing her parents here was an act of grace, a way for them to settle down in a city she would feel much safer in.

How was it then that they arrived to find this chaos?

"We should turn back," her mom said, pulling at the braid in her hair, a nervous tic she often displayed in such moments.

"Mom, I'm sorry, but we have ammo. Guns." Robin went to the rail of the airship and looked out, trying to get a better view of the approaching army. "If we're right about what this is, I'd say they'll need our help."

"I'm not putting my baby in harm's way," her dad said. "I won't, I—"

"Dad." Robin smiled, showing her fangs and letting her red eyes glow. "I hardly need your protection anymore."

"Don't do that."

She shrugged, but felt a pang of guilt. "I'm just trying to show you I'm not your little baby anymore."

He scoffed and tried to smile, but then his face crumbled into sorrow-filled love. "Even if you take that whole army all by yourself, even if you're named empress of the world, you'll always be my little girl."

She rolled her eyes, even if she did appreciate it. You didn't go on a quest to find your parents and worry every second of the day about whether they were alive or not and then not enjoy their cheesiness.

"Do what you need to do, dear," her mom said, laying a hand on her shoulder and a kiss on her head. "We support you."

The wrinkles and gray hair showed that her mother had aged beyond her years in her time as a slave for the Toro bandits, but Robin still saw the younger Mom in there, smiling out with a zest for life.

"We'll turn this world around yet," Robin replied.

"Off the starboard bow," one of the men shouted. "Incoming."

They all rushed over and, sure enough, one Pod was racing toward them, several following in its wake.

"Hostiles?" the man asked.

"No," Robin replied, as if she could sense Valerie there. "I don't think so."

With a *swoosh* of air the first Pod came alongside the moving airship, slowing to move at the same pace. The door opened to reveal Valerie in the pilot's seat.

"What in the holy hell brought you all this far south at the worst possible moment?"

Robin raised a hand, shouting back over the wind, "That would be me."

Valerie laughed and said something to the guy next to her, then hopped up onto the seat and jumped. For a moment the Pod behind her lost control as the passenger leaped to fly it, but then it recovered to head back toward New York. The rest moved up beside the ships, forming an escort into the city.

"Mom, Dad." Robin gestured to Valerie, who had just landed on the ship and was now standing next to her. "You remember my good friend Valerie."

Valerie shook their hands and then hugged Robin tightly, lifting her off the deck. "It's good to see you!"

"You too, as long as you don't crush my ribs." Robin laughed as her feet touched down again. "I'll be honest." She gestured to the army visible not so far outside the walls now. "This isn't exactly the reception I was hoping for."

"Hey, we went all out, just for you."

Robin laughed, but her parents were frowning, apparently not so amused.

"Are we going to be safe here?" her dad asked.

Valerie nodded. "I won't allow a single citizen of New York to be hurt. We're going after these attackers, and we're going to strike fast. I trust," she turned to Robin, "you're in?"

Ignoring the sigh from her mother, Robin nodded. "You bet your ass I am."

Her dad shook his head. "Language."

Robin and Valerie chuckled, but quickly hid their smiles. It was a weird feeling, being around her parents and Val. Like they were two school girls being careful not to get into trouble.

That was a sensation she hadn't had much of a chance to experience. She liked it.

"Let's bring these ships in and get to work," Valerie said. Again she shook hands with Robin's parents, adding, "It was truly great to meet you. I look forward to having a chance to talk more when this is all over."

"Us too," Robin's mom replied, and her dad nodded.

"I have a lot to catch you up on," Valerie told Robin. "Over wine at Sandra's?"

Robin considered that, then nodded slowly. "As long as we both agree everything's as we left it, as we discussed."

Valerie nodded, her eyes conveying no hint of remorse, even if she was feeling it. *Maybe her journey to Europe put her in a different mindset*, Robin thought. Maybe she truly *was* okay with the idea that Robin felt they were better off as just friends and teammates; that all the romance stuff got in the way of their focus.

Or maybe she was just a damn good actress. Either way, Robin smiled and said, "It's a d-deal." She caught herself, having almost said "date." She hoped her friend hadn't noticed. Old habits were hard to break.

Valerie put her hand on her sword hilt and turned to look at the army. "But first we have ourselves a date with death, and I've promised to bring her a mighty large bouquet of souls tonight."

"If you'll excuse us," Robin's dad said, giving her a smile and Valerie a wary look before departing with his wife at his arm.

"They don't like me?" Valerie asked.

"You did just talk about death and killing a bunch of people, pretty much."

Valerie cocked her head, considering that. "Huh. I guess normal people don't like that."

"I guess not." Robin flung the corner of her jacket back to reveal her own sword—a pirate blade left over from their northern adventures. "Good thing I'm not normal."

"We're well beyond that," Valerie replied with a laugh, and they both watched in silence as the army advanced.

A chill breeze worked its way through Espinoza's camouflaged wind jacket, sending goose bumps along his arms and neck. The cold didn't bother him, and neither did the sight of the army taking up an assault position outside the walls. He was ready for them, and knew that once the fighting started his adrenalin would kick in, his instincts take over.

Fighters were there with him, including the one they called Jackson and the El Diablo guy Arturo.

"We'll take that position," Espinoza stated, pointing to a section of wall behind him. It was front and center, but had good cover. A perfect spot to dole out ultimate damage without having to receive too much in return.

"Agreed." Jackson leaned against the wall considering their situation, then hefted his rifle and aimed at the enemy. "You think we could take out a couple from here?"

"Fuck it," Arturo replied, moving to a mounted SAW machine gun and motioning to the man behind him. "Feed this beast."

"We'll rile them up," Espinoza countered. "Are we sure we want to do that?"

"Better to fight them on our terms," Jackson countered, "than sitting around here waiting."

"You see a kid walking up to you with a stick, hit him in the face with a rock before he's close enough to strike." Espinoza lost himself in a moment, memories of blood, adults yelling, him shrugging like it was nothing and walking away from the would-be attacker kid. Even at nine years of age, he'd known fighting was in his blood.

He became aware that while other men and women were chatting and preparing on the wall, the group around him was staring at him.

"Violent past?"

"We were all kids once," he countered. "My childhood just happened to take place mostly in the Wastelands."

"What we call the 'Badlands,'" Jackson offered. "And yeah, I see how that could make a kid do things that might cause them to get creepy-ass looks in their eyes as adults."

Everyone laughed, including Espinoza.

"Hey, be happy I'm on your side," he replied.

"I am, you can count on that." Jackson winked and added, "What'd'ya say we get to work then, huh?"

Espinoza nodded, then turned to one of his men, the one they called "Duckhole," or sometimes just "Ducky." Why? Because he had a nice sniper rifle, the kind that, when paired with him, would send a shot right through a duck's butthole from nearly two miles away. The enemy was definitely closer than that.

"Ducky," he said, motioning the man up.

The others made room for him, though that didn't take much. Despite being badass he was a scrawny guy, standing not much taller than his sniper rifle when set vertically.

"Sup, boss?" Ducky wasn't much for formalities.

"You want to pop their cherry?"

Duckhole glanced at the men around him, then looked back at Espinoza. "Not particularly."

"A badass, but not too bright," Espinoza quipped over his shoulder to the others. "No, you stupid piece of meat, *theirs*." This time he motioned to the enemy and Duckhole smiled wide, revealing his lack of a left incisor.

"You want a show, is that it?" Duckhole asked. He hefted the sniper rifle and took his position on the wall, making a few adjustments while they waited. "Watch and learn."

"Ready?" Espinoza asked the others. "When he hits his target, let loose."

"Fuckin' A," Arturo replied, clamping the ammo belt into the SAW.

"Three, two…." No count of one, just the explosion of the bullet leaving the chamber and the sound of cursing as it met its mark. A figure dropped and Arturo opened up on the rest, casings flying out to the side.

"Get some!" Espinoza shouted, pulling up his rifle to take aim. Only, as he did so, a sound came from behind them.

He turned to see several Pods flying, five by his count, and then saw Valerie open the door. She stood there with an automatic machine gun, smiling as she passed, and then started singing—if you could call it that.

"Na-na-na-na-naaaa, na. Na-na-na-na-naaa, na. Na-na-na-na-naaaaa-na." Then she joined in the fun, others opening up from the Pods too, riddling the attackers with bullets as they flew past them.

The men and women below were scrambling to form ranks and return fire, but many of them were being plowed down.

"Get some!" Espinoza shouted after them, knowing Garcia was up there and, for a moment, envying him. Charging out into battle like that—was there any better feeling? The rush of the thought sent a new vigor through him and he leaned on the wall now, using it to steady his rifle as he blasted out round after round.

Cammie and Royland were at the wall when they saw the Pods fly out, and she turned to Royland with what she was sure must've come across as a mischievous smile.

"We're not gonna let them have all the fun, are we?" Cammie asked.

He rolled his eyes. "Your definition of fun varies vastly from mine at times."

"Well, we're just going to have to work on shared interests, I guess."

"And now's one of those times?"

She nodded innocently and pulled out two short blades. Once they had been concealed as kali fighting sticks, but not anymore. It was a good thing she had found them after all this time, since she wouldn't think of running out there with any other weapon. Fighting as a human was sometimes preferable in that she could continue conversing with others on her team and didn't have to bite her enemies.

As the fusillade continued outside, she took off for the steps and shouted, "Open that gate!"

The guard glared at her. "We've been given orders."

"Open the damned gate!" she repeated. "And then close it again, understood?"

He hesitated, but at a red glow from Royland's eyes he moved to do as she commanded, shouting at his buddy to get the gate open.

A moment later the two were out, running to join in the fun. Up above the Pods were circling the enemy for a second time, shots traveling in both directions.

"Hold that gate," another voice called, and Cammie turned to see Arturo and Espinoza and his team following them out.

"Not a fan of the safety of walls?" Espinoza shouted after them—they had already gone a good distance.

"It takes away all the excitement," she called back. "Try to keep up. I'm not babysitting out here!"

With that she turned with Royland and continued the charge on the enemy, reaching them just as the Pods above were coming in for the third sweep.

CHAPTER FOURTEEN

Outside New York

Everyone cheered as the Pod came around for a third pass, Valerie leaning out through the open door. She held her position with one hand and the machine gun with the other and opened up on the enemy below.

Bright lights flashed in the night, her enemy falling in their wake. At the edge of the group she saw fighters charging into the enemy ranks and a new front to the fight breaking out. A second glance showed Cammie, Royland, Espinoza, and others moving in from the city.

Those crazy sons of bitches.

She laughed, thinking of the best way to cover them—if they even needed it.

"Best. Night. Ever," Garcia said, pulling back in from the other side to refill his rifle while Robin switched back in.

A torrent of bullets pinging off the Pod came in reply.

"Put her in dodge mode," Robin commanded. "RPG!"

"How the hell do they have RPGs?" Garcia shouted, sounding more pissed than curious.

"Doesn't matter right now," Valerie said, taking the controls back. She spun the Pod away from the incoming projectile toward the back of the forces, where some had yet to join in the fight. "Don't shoot. I have an idea."

She stood, leaning out of the window as Fred held the controls, and, as the RPG flew past, she shouted at the top of her amplified voice, "This doesn't have to end with your death! Your lives matter. They shouldn't just be thrown away. In New York, we know that. We know you are a mighty enemy, but you could be an even mightier ally! You will be welcome just like so many who've come before you, and—"

As she spoke, a bullet dinged off the Pod inches from her head. Two shots rang out in response; Garcia had taken out the shooter.

Valerie sighed. "Don't fire on us and we won't fire on you. Lay down your arms if you can; flee and come back later, or fight those who would force you to fight against your will!"

A moment of silence followed, broken only by the skirmish Royland and Cammie were part of.

"You have to the count of three," she added. "One... Two... Three."

On three, chaos broke out below because some actually did listen to her. An outer group started making for the hills, while others turned on the people next to them. One group began chasing the ones who had run, shooting at them.

"Get as many of them as you can," Valerie commanded, pointing to the shooters. "We want our people to know we have their backs."

Her Pod maneuvered to defend the ones who had switched sides and the other Pods followed.

"You missed this, didn't you?" she called to Robin, who was leaning out the back window, rifle up and about to shoot.

"Doling out justice and fighting for freedom?" She laughed as she fired several rounds. "You're damn right I did."

"Then you're gonna *love* this." Valerie suddenly jolted the Pod to the side, putting them directly in the line of fire, and leaped out. She hit the ground rolling, and when she landed only spared a second to see that Robin had followed before she took off toward the enemy. Her rifle was up and she took down as many as she could while she ran, but then she slung it over her torso and drew her sword.

The Pod flew over them and most of the fighters directed their fire on it, apparently not realizing what a threat Valerie was. And now that she had Robin at her side? Double whammy.

The two ran through the crowd of those firing at them. Valerie *pushed* a wave of fear, causing many to stumble or turn in confusion, and then she was upon them.

Spraying blood, bodies in heaps, and Valerie and Robin in the midst of it all like a dance of death.

For a moment the enemy parted and Valerie caught a glimpse of Cammie. The two smiled and waved as if they had just spotted each other at a shopping mall, and then got back to it.

From the crowd, one large man lumbered forward and unslung a crude ax. He threw it at her and began to run when she dodged, transforming into a bear as he did. Two others came up behind him and transformed into wolves. Now she was excited for the challenge.

She hefted her sword and charged, surprised to see Robin careening around from her right, big ax in hand. Apparently she'd caught it or recovered it, and now meant to place it in its owner's skull.

Fine by her. Valerie made a sideways pounce that put her in line with one of the wolves just as the bear stumbled past her, ax cleaving one of its legs. One wolf leaped for her, the other cutting across and coming for her legs when she stepped back to brace herself for impact.

Since her weight was already distributed, she couldn't move before the wolf clamped down on her calf. However, she was able to duck and the other wolf went flying over her. Before it had a chance to recover, she dropped her sword and had managed the grab the closer wolf and pull its jaws apart, forcing it to release her leg. She didn't stop there, though, and when jaw bones splintered the wolf fell back whimpering. The whimpers became screams as it transformed into a hideous sight.

The second wolf went for her shoulder and she fell back with it, holding it off as it scratched. Out of the corner of her eye she saw Robin deliver the final blow to the large bear, ax plunging halfway through its neck as it fell with a thud onto a pile of corpses.

Not wanting to be outdone, Valerie thrust up with her hips and kicked the wolf off, then spun, grabbed her sword, and tossed it. The blade impaled the wolf right between the eyes.

The enemy around them had watched in stunned silence, and many were now turning to run or get out of harm's way rather than bending the knee. Everyone who remained, however, began firing at once.

While Valerie might've been able to dodge all of the bullets by herself, she knew that Robin wasn't quite there yet. Instead of protecting herself she ran for Robin and dove, pulling her behind by the bear's corpse and out of harm's way.

"I didn't need your help," Robin stated, furious.

"Well, you're going to get it anyway," Valerie countered. "Cover me."

"What?"

"Now!" Valerie ran back out, heading for her sword as bullets shot past, narrowly missing her.

Robin returned fire, since she had thankfully picked up one of the enemy's fallen rifles and figured out quickly what "cover me" meant in this context.

Scooping up the sword, Valerie slid and dug it into the ground so that she had suddenly changed directions. She pulled it free and charged the shooters, smiling with anticipation. Nobody was allowed to march on her city, try to shoot her friends, or stand there trying to kill her.

Not today. *Not ever.*

As she connected with the first group two bullets hit her side and left arm, but only grazing shots. It hurt, but wasn't enough to mess up her form. A thrust here, a swipe there, and soon she was stepping through them in an old-world kata, a beautiful martial pattern taught to her by sword masters back in Old France.

A click sounded behind her and she turned, ready to attack, but saw Robin there, having just dropped someone by biting into their neck and drinking. Valerie often forgot that her friend still needed to be replenished when expending this much energy.

"Holding up?" she shouted over the noise of gunshots and more enemies charging them.

Robin nodded, took a deep breath, and then stood at Valerie's side, ready. "Me? I'm just getting started."

"That's what I like to hear."

The attack came and they met it head on, soon creating a spiral of corpses around them that began to form a barrier to further attacks.

Cammie was fighting to reach Valerie and Robin, but the closer she got, the more she realized that maybe being too close might be a bad idea. Those two were like forces of nature, tearing through everything in their path.

What if she was the next thing in their path and they didn't realize it was her?

Espinoza and his team were doing a good job of laying down suppressive fire while most of the enemy was trying to get at the vampires and the Weres on the field. When one of them turned to throw a grenade at the soldiers Cammie moved fast, plowing through him and then using the butt-end of her short-sword to hit the grenade like a baseball. It went flying and exploded over a group of the attacker's buddies, sending shrapnel down upon them.

She looked around for more grenades to throw their way, eyes wide at the sight of two more on the man's vest.

"Fuck yeah!" she shouted, though Royland gave her a skeptical glance. "What?"

"Just be careful."

"Oh, come on." She took one, pulled the pin, and lobbed it. "What's the point of playtime if you have to be careful?"

KA-BOOM!

She took the other, smiled wide, and rolled it like a bowling ball into a trio that had just decided she was their point of focus instead of Valerie. The explosion shook the air, followed by body parts raining down on them.

An eye landed on Royland's shoulder, which he quickly brushed off.

"Dammit, Cammie!"

"For a blood-sucking vampire," she replied, pulling out her blades again, "you sure can be a prude."

With a giggle, she ran into the wall of fighters, who were covered in blood and looking her way in disgust. Sure, maybe she was a tad drunk on adrenalin, but this shit was fun. She wasn't about to let anyone kill her buzz. Anyone except for Valerie, apparently.

Moments after Cammie reached this group and took two out Valerie and Robin appeared, cutting down a few more each. Before Cammie moved past them to attack she stopped, heart sinking at the sight. Everyone who remained was dropping their weapons or running. *Lame*, she thought as she turned back to find Royland.

At the sight of the carnage Valerie was causing among her enemies more of them surrendered, dropping their weapons or turning on those beside them.

Soon there was silence. Valerie stopped, turning to Robin with a look of curiosity. Sure enough, the fighting was over as quickly as that. Many lay dead and others knelt with hands out or behind their heads, staring at them in terror. Some groups were visible in distance running for the hills, and she imagined these were mostly enemies who would regroup with the rest of Lady Woo's forces.

"The fight isn't over," she said to Micky as he and Garcia exited the Pod and approached.

He shook his head.

Turning to one of the men on his knees, Valerie knelt and *pushed* enough fear to make him talk, though she wasn't sure it was even necessary.

"The rest of her forces?" Valerie asked.

"Her?" the man asked, voice trembling.

"Lady Woo. Isn't she in charge?"

He considered that, eyes moving back and forth. "I...suppose? No one is really in charge, not of the whole group. But she and the other group the leaders held back, yes. I think they were hoping we could take the city without them getting their hands dirty."

"Sounds about right," Micky replied with a grunt.

"And everyone here, you are ready to switch sides?" Valerie asked.

The man in front of her nodded, others doing the same. But one thing was clear—they were terrified. With a sigh, she walked over to the Pod and hopped on top so she could see them all.

"There's something I want to make very clear right now," she stated, loudly enough for all to hear. "Whatever you've heard about us, throw it out right now. Our city is thriving because we have gotten rid of prejudice. We've cast aside fear and hatred and embraced a world where we will all be able to live in peace."

Robin stepped up now too, waiting for a nod from Valerie. When she received it, she turned to the crowd. "When I lived in the Badlands I was taken from my home, forced to do things I didn't want to do, hurt people who didn't deserve it. The kind of pain I went through, emotional and physical—none of us should have to experience that. Valerie helped me through it, and we can help all of you."

Valerie nodded. "But only if you help yourselves. Stand up and throw aside the chains laid on you by others. You might not have felt trapped—hell, maybe you're here fighting for supposed freedom—but the bonds were what held you to a world where violence is acceptable. The Badlands need to be cleaned up so that every one of you knows you're safe and secure. Never again should you have to worry about your son, daughter, mother, brother, sister, father... Did I get them all?"

Robin chuckled. "Good enough."

Valerie took a moment to look over them, stopping to nod at Cammie and the others who had helped and were now watching and listening.

Turning back to the men and women they had been fighting mere moments before, she continued, "None of you should have to ever worry about a loved one being hurt again!" Valerie jumped down and started walking among them. "Stand with us! Stand! Tell Lady Woo and all the rest out there that we don't accept the status quo. We fight for change! For an evolution of society! Are you with me?"

"We're with you!" a man said, standing, motioning to those around him to do the same.

"As are we!" a woman shouted from the other side, her people standing too. Soon everyone was standing, and they were clearly into it.

Valerie nodded to each of them in turn.

"They will return, as you know. When that happens, we'll ask for help to keep them back, to prove that you are trustworthy. When we return, if that has been the case, you may join our city."

Murmurs of agreement rose from the crowd.

"Good," Valerie said, moving back to the Pod. "We're going to go deal with the leaders and anyone else left standing in our way. Welcome, ladies and gentlemen, to the winning side."

"You think they'll fight with us and not turn tail at the last minute?" Garcia asked.

"After what they just witnessed," Valerie interjected, "they'll fight with us. They'd be too scared not to."

Cammie appeared from her right, having just jogged over. "Nice speech. Here's the deal: we'll babysit your new pets."

"What?"

"These ones," Cammie said with a smile, motioning to the new fighters with her blade. "I figure I'm out here anyway; might as well make use of the moment. Test them, make sure they know what they're getting into. And if the others return, we'll lead this group against them."

Valerie nodded her approval. "You're really into this whole taking-charge thing now, huh?"

"Apparently. Just hurry your asses back so you don't miss the fun."

"Right. You'd probably call sneaking into the enemy camp to take out their leaders fun."

Cammie thought about it, then smiled. "Wanna switch?"

"Ha! You wish!" Valerie winked and gave Royland a nod. "Keep them out of trouble, Royland. You're the old man here."

"Thanks for the reminder."

When she reached the Pod and Micky, Valerie asked, "You ready to show us where this Lady Woo's fortress is?"

He nodded and soon they were in the air, heading for the final showdown.

Valerie glanced at Robin as they flew, the two of them smiling and sharing that moment as if the rest of the world were invisible.

"You made the right choice, you know, coming back," Valerie said.

"I know." Robin leaned back and closed her eyes, then opened them and laughed. "I just keep seeing you out there kicking ass. It's like you've gotten better, if that was possible. You were amazing in Toro, but this was like the ultimate Valerie. It was beautiful."

"It" being the key word there. Not "you." Valerie's smile faltered and Robin noticed, but before either could address the issue or even have time to feel awkward, Garcia leaned forward and said, "I thought Micky's moves were pretty beautiful too. You all see the way his massive finger pulled the trigger? Huh? You see that?"

"Shut up," Valerie countered as she pushed him back.

Micky laughed and poked Garcia in the chest with that massive finger. "Hey, pal, this finger happens to have been solely responsible for at least ten evil assholes dying so far tonight. It plans on taking down about a bajillion more. So, yeah, you'd better damn well recognize it as a thing of beauty."

Garcia grabbed the finger and analyzed it. "You know, now that you mention it…" He couldn't go on, but just cracked up.

"You're cheery for having just served on the equivalent of a massive firing squad," Fred noted. "I'm not sure I could do it and smile after."

"What, take down those pricks?" Garcia asked. "Let me put it this way, buddy. Each of them would've happily taken those weapons of theirs and strolled through New York mowing down anyone they saw. Man, woman, child—anyone. You're telling me it doesn't bring a smile to your face to stop that from happening?"

Fred just gulped, eyes darting around and finally landing on Valerie.

"Nope, no help from me on this one," she replied.

"I don't care if I have to pull their guts out with my bare hands or chomp down on their still-beating hearts," Garcia continued, "if that's what it takes to end them, to protect the ones we love and the ones who aren't able to protect themselves."

"Damn straight," Micky added.

"You're with me on this?"

"Hell yes, I am. I've seen too many people who didn't deserve to die get mowed down to prove someone else's power. Or, you know what? To show they could. Some of these motherfuckers just shoot people because they can, because that's the world we live in, especially in the Badlands. Not again. No way. We're changing it."

"You bet your ass we are," Valerie interjected. "Tonight, it ends."

"Bless your heart," Micky said, nodding. "Shit, if I could go back and tear each of those bastards apart before they had the chance to do what they did, if I had the power to see if someone was evil and act on it, imagine what I'd do!"

"You mean punish them before they'd done anything wrong because you had the power to know they would?" Robin asked.

"That's right. You would too, wouldn't you?"

Robin looked puzzled, then shook her head. "I'd always wonder if I was insane, living some delusional fantasy. Here I'd be, killing all these innocents because my messed-up head convinced me it was the right thing to do. In reality, I'd be no better than they had the potential to become."

"Well, if you think of it that way it's less fun," Micky replied with a pout.

"Plus," Valerie interjected, "what's to say that isn't the case now? Maybe you've imagined me and I'm just some weird part of your psyche you use to justify everything you've done, but all the outsiders just see you, not some crazy bitch?"

"You want to know how I know you're real?" Robin asked.

She turned and punched Valerie in the arm, causing her to yelp and swerve the Pod. "See, I didn't feel that at all, and it messed with your flying even. I rest my case."

"Technically, if you were h—"

"Nope." She folded her arms. "I'm done with that conversation. Point is, we stopped a lot of bad people from doing bad things tonight, and worse in days ahead. For that, I'm glad."

"Fuckin' A," Garcia replied, then let out a loud, *"Get some!"*

Micky threw his head back, laughing. "I love this son of a bitch right here."

Fred made a disgusted sound.

"Too much testosterone back there for you?" Robin asked.

"Call it what you want," he countered. "I'm just not convinced death should ever be surrounded by this attitude."

"Says the man who was on Lady Woo's side." Garcia frowned suddenly. "Or...still is?"

"Shut up. You know that's not true."

Garcia nodded. "I *believe* it's not true. Can't rule out the possibility, though."

"Fine...say I was. You'd just kill me as soon as you saw me on the battlefield, right? And it's not like I could bring Lady Woo any news other than telling her the people coming for her are insane, right?"

"Good points."

"If it helps," Valerie noted, "I can read emotions. It's not exactly like reading thoughts, but I can generally tell when someone is lying, scared, in love..."

That left a very awkward silence in the Pod.

"Um, your point?" Micky finally asked.

"Right. I mean, I can tell Fred's legit because I can read his emotions. You all are lucky. Some vampires, or at least one or two that I know of, can actually read thoughts."

"Yuck! You get in my mind, I'm going to...to..." Garcia scratched his head. "Okay, there's not much I could do to you, but

I would certainly do something. Start gossip about you having bad breath or something. Blood breath, yeah!"

"For the record," Valerie replied. "It's been a bit since I drank blood, and I've managed to keep my breath quite fresh. You know how your stomachs have all those problems with gas and whatnot, giving you bad breath and farts? Well, not a problem."

"Bullshit," Micky countered with a large laugh. "You're saying you don't fart?"

She thought about it and shook her head. "Can't say I remember the last time I did."

"This is too much," Robin interrupted, burying her face in her hand. "Can we just get there already so we can start killing?"

"Actually," Valerie glanced back at Micky and pointed out the window. "That our destination?"

He leaned forward, then pulled back as if they could see him. "Shit, yes. Get her down, get her down."

She figured they were lucky to have been flying at night without lights, or they would've likely been spotted.

Mentally pulling herself together and getting ready for the fight ahead, trying to pretend she hadn't just been talking about farts with these guys, she maneuvered the Pod toward the ground.

CHAPTER FIFTEEN

The Fortress

At the point where the hills met in a downward slope, the walls of Lady Woo's fortress visible just past the tree line, the three Pods touched down.

Valerie turned to Fred in the back. "Are you sure you don't want any of us to go with you?"

"It would look more suspicious," he replied. "They would be wary of me approaching with an outsider."

"Fine. But if you get into any trouble—"

"What? Click my heels together and say your name three times or something?" He chuckled.

"I was going to say run like hell, but you could try that too. Who knows, right?"

"I'll see you all soon enough," he said, moving to the Pod they had all decided he would take. This way, as long as he didn't crash, he could get close to each place he was going, walk in and try to convince them to join, then move on to the next.

Valerie and her companions marched up the hill for a better look at their objective. While Fred was out there seeing who he could persuade to switch sides, they would lead an assault on this place.

It looked like an old hospital, or maybe an insane asylum. Either way, it had barred windows and tall walls. Cement slabs were arranged out front, and it was clear that this building had been attacked at least once in its past.

As the Pod behind them took off Valerie glanced at Micky, Garcia, and Robin.

"That talk earlier about being crazy…think this is the type of place they would've thrown you into?"

Robin frowned. "If we walk in there only to find that I'm actually strapped to a chair getting electric-shock therapy and you're all figments of my imagination out here, representations of my doctors or something… I'm just warning you now, I will kill you all and break out."

"Well then, let's hope you're not crazy and this is really happening," Micky replied with a chuckle.

"Want me to pinch you so you can see if you're sleeping or not?" Garcia asked her.

"You pinch me, you get a vampire fist in the face," she replied. "Plus, I've never really bought into that whole 'pinch to see if you're sleeping' thing. In a dream, wouldn't I just dream the pinch and then I would feel it in the dream? I mean, who thought of that, anyway?"

"I can't argue that."

"How about we not argue at all and just get to work?" Micky offered. When no one had an argument against that, he smiled. "Right. I've never been here, but I've heard of this place. The indies call it Bonus Tirith, though I'm not sure why. It's their fortress, their agreed-upon stronghold if they should ever face a unified threat."

"Which means they're fucking idiots," Garcia said with a laugh. "I mean, right?"

"All of them together in one place…" Valerie shrugged. "Seems that way."

"From your point of view, maybe," Garcia admitted. "But when you think about the fact that they've rigged this place with weapons they've found over the years and that their contingency plan involves a group of vampires and Weres standing guard, it might not seem like such a bad idea."

"Until someone of Valerie's power comes along," Robin pointed out.

"That's the flaw," Micky conceded. "Of course, since they've never experienced anyone of Valerie's power, it might have seemed like a very smart move until now."

"I can still be killed, you guys." Valerie glanced down at where her shirt was torn but the skin had healed from being kissed by a bullet earlier. "At least, I think so."

"No better time than now to find out," Micky said with a grin.

"Not funny." Robin pointed at Valerie and added, "Don't you dare die. You do, and I swear by all that's holy I'm coming after you to kick your ass."

"Deal." Valerie bit her lip, then nodded. "Okay, it's settled. I go in alone, you guys cover me. You hear the shooting stop and don't see any sign of me, you come in after me."

"Perfect, except of course I'm coming too." Robin checked her weapons, not even bothering to see if she got a response to that.

"I can't put you at risk," Valerie said when nobody else spoke. "Not after meeting Mr. and Mrs. Robin."

"Their names are Mom and Dad, and don't worry, I know you won't let me die."

"Thanks for the vote of confidence."

She was about to argue further, but she knew Robin too well and that it wouldn't work. With a sigh, she nodded.

"Best method of attack?" she asked Micky.

"You're letting her go, then?" Garcia asked, skeptical.

"She's not my mom," Robin countered.

"I mean, you're barely an adult."

Robin turned on him, but Valerie got between the two. "First, no fighting between my crew."

"We're your crew now?" he asked.

"Yes, you are. Second, you want to question someone on the team, do it on your own time, and take it up with me first. I hear another comment like 'She's barely an adult' or 'but he's only a man, not even modified,' because let's be honest, both of you guys are that, I'm kicking some ass. Got it?" She turned back to Micky, not even waiting for a response. She knew they got it. "Now, best method of attack? You have to have heard something we can use here."

He pursed his lips, staring at the ghostlike building, its white walls gleaming in the moonlight. "Not much, to be honest. Except from before; they say there was a massive breakout from this place. Soon after the Great Collapse, local groups started throwing their prisoners in here. I mean for some time too, that lasted. Kids were born and raised there. But one day they rose up, broke out, and came back to slaughter their captors. Only, it didn't stop there. They moved on to the surrounding towns and cities and massacred anyone who wouldn't accept them as their rulers, then—"

"Micky," Valerie interrupted. "I asked for a plan of attack, not ghost stories."

He shrugged. "Not as much of a ghost story as you think. Lady Woo was one of them, the stories say. She was only a child, but even then she was crazy as all get-out. Stories say she was the one to kill most of the children. She insisted, and when one of the adults in the group questioned her, she grabbed his gun and killed him too. Crazy little kid. Crazier adult."

"And we've let people like this survive?"

"Apparently."

"Fine, so they broke out." Valerie turned back to the hospital, assessing the grounds. "Where?"

"Around back. They've covered it up by now, I'm sure, but it's gotta be more vulnerable than the rest of the place. Plus, they might not have bothered to do much with it, figuring their attackers wouldn't know the stories. After all, they killed everyone involved, so only insiders knew."

Valerie wasn't the only one who did a doubletake at that. He shrugged. "Pops. He had his history, that's for sure."

"Damn," Garcia said.

Robin nodded. "People nowadays...like a box of crackers."

"Never know what you're gonna get?"

"What? No, you're gonna get a bunch of stale ones. Some have been eaten by mice, some have mouse shit on them. You might get lucky if you find a couple that still have the taste of salt to them, but otherwise, you might as well just make your own crackers from scratch."

"Robin, what the hell are you talking about?" Valerie asked.

"Sorry, I'm realizing I'm hungry."

"And your hunger makes you talk about moldy crackers?" Garcia laughed. "Some appetite."

"I never said moldy. I don't think that happens to crackers."

"Team, focus." Valerie breathed, reminding herself to set the boundaries early with her next team. "What else did Pops tell you, Micky?"

"He talked about being wet and—or am I mixing this up with a story he used to say he heard from a friend?—about the smell."

"Oh, hell no," Valerie pulled back, scrunching her nose. "They went through the sewage pipes, didn't they?"

"Yeah!"

"We're not doing that." She turned to Robin. "Agreed?"

"Damn straight."

"Yeah, forget this." Valerie stood and adjusted her sword belt and felt for the pistol at her thigh, then realized it might be a good idea to see if it was loaded. "I love this whole planning thing, but here's the deal. We're just going to kick their asses.

Robin, stick with me but stay behind so I can charge up; you make sure they don't surround me. I don't want you getting shot because I dodged a bullet. I want the bullet hitting the guy behind me, then you jumping in to kill his girlfriend. Got it?"

She nodded.

"Wait, you're just going to charge in there?" Micky frowned. "What about catching them off-guard? Being sneaky?"

"Wouldn't they expect that?"

He considered, then nodded. "I suppose so."

"Exactly. So mine is the better way to catch them off-guard." She beamed. "Any questions?"

"We just sit here, ready to shoot anything that looks out of place?" Garcia asked.

"Sounds like we all know what we're doing."

"Only one problem." Garcia pulled his rifle to his shoulder and spun. "There's a whole shit-ton of things looking out of place right now."

Valerie took a sniff and cursed herself for not paying attention. Now that she smelled them, she glanced around and saw them too. Various figures were moving in on them. They must've triggered some sort of sensor or something on their way in, or simply been spotted after all. Of course, if they had vampires and Weres—which they apparently did—flying at night wouldn't have done much to conceal the Pod.

"New plan, then," Valerie said.

"Fight like crazy and hope we survive?" Garcia asked.

"You know this one?" She smiled, but nodded at the Pod. "I don't want you two getting hit, so take cover in there and shoot from within. It's bullet-resistant."

"That's comforting."

"Robin and I will do our thing from out here. Go!"

They broke for it and Valerie spun, ready to make a move on whatever group would come first. A rustling of trees sounded and something was moving, smashing through them. Three large wolves, leaping from the ground to push off trees, moved to avoid the bullets that started fanning out from Garcia and Micky's direction.

A closer scent caught her attention—a vampire, at least one. But it seemed to be right where she was. She spun, not seeing anything, and then realized her mistake. When she turned to look up, she saw him.

It was a slender vampire, his teeth gleaming in the night, his eyes wide with curiosity at seeing her.

Still, he didn't hesitate. In an instant he had leaped for her, a long sharp metal rod in his hands. He attempted to spear her heart, then aimed the spike for the soft section under her jaw. Spinning out of his way, she saw the Weres arrive and Robin take out the first one with a series of blasts from her rifle.

The distraction was enough to give the vampire the advantage, and his next strike caught Valerie in the thigh. She grunted in pain and in one swift motion pulled it out, flipped it into the next Were's torso, pulled her sword, and turned to the vampire.

"Come on, you sonofabitch."

"I could've killed you," he said, "But you interest me. I find myself wanting to know more about you. For example, what do you think you're doing here?"

"Stopping Lady Woo and the rest of them. You?"

He smiled. "Defending Lady Woo and the rest of them."

"Will you stop talking and kill him already?!" Robin shouted, doing a damn good job of keeping the Weres at bay. Hey, she was doing a great job, so what was the hurry?

"Guess that makes us mortal enemies then, huh?" Valerie said to the vampire, putting on a fake pout. "Our chances of being each other's eternal soul mate are crushed."

"Oh, you took my hitting you the wrong way," he replied with a sneer. "*Hitting* you, not hitting *on* you. See the difference?"

She actually smiled now, stepping aside as a dead Were flew

past. "Pity. I'd hate to kill the one Forsaken with a sense of humor."

He laughed, giving only a slight glance at the dead Were at his feet. "And honestly, I'd hate to die. But we do what we must."

"Indeed." She hesitated. "You don't have to fight me, you know. You could still turn and walk away."

"Afraid I can't," he replied, and charged.

She decided to give him a fair chance, sheathing her sword and taking him on in hand-to-hand combat. Behind her Robin was shouting something about her finally getting into the action. It was hard to not make a witty comeback to that, but she decided to keep it to herself. Sometimes it was best to focus on the fight, and now was one of those times.

He attempted to grab her by the shirt and slam her into a nearby tree, but she used her leg behind his as leverage to spin him around. Together they hit the ground, where she brought her elbow into first his nose, then twisted and brought her other elbow down hard on his groin.

She quickly rolled away and onto her feet.

He stood up bloody and wincing, so that when he charged her it was full of anger and therefore careless.

A simple sidestep and strike sent him headfirst into a nearby tree. More forms had appeared around them, she noticed, and now gunshots sounded on both sides. *Damn, so much for the element of surprise.*

As the vampire stumbled to recover, bullets riddled his body and he fell over. Valerie scampered up a tree and then dove, tackling a shooter and bringing up his rifle to crack the skull of the person next to him. Next she appropriated both their rifles and mowed down a line of people nearby. She saw her friends shooting from the Pod, taking out more would-be attackers.

Robin stomped over, the dead wolves behind her, and she looked pissed.

"You hurt?" Valerie asked, suddenly worried.

"Only by the fact that you'd rather talk and flirt than get shit done," Robin replied. She ducked slightly as more shots came, but the return fire was soon stopped by Garcia and Micky.

"So…you're saying you'd like to go ahead and attack the fortress now?"

Robin frowned. "If you mean run into that hospital, guns blazing? Then yes."

"Grab some weapons," Valerie said, still holding her two rifles, "and let's go!"

Together, each holding two rifles and ready to blast some evil bastards, the two vampire ladies ran toward the old hospital. There was no chance of a surprise attack so they let out their war cries, Valerie *pushing* fear into those within, and prepared for the worst.

CHAPTER SIXTEEN

The Fortress

The attack on the fortress caught Valerie off-guard—she had really thought they would just run up, kick down some doors, and kill people like crazy. Those things would come, but not until they figured out how to deal with the deathtraps waiting out front.

When these leaders had set this place up as a fallback they hadn't been kidding around. The first clue came when Robin stepped on a land mine. If it weren't for her vampire speed she definitely would've lost a leg. As it was, she was hit in the back by a hunk of debris. The explosion signaled to those within that they were close, and immediately alarms went off. Gun ports were opened and a new barrage of bullets rained down. When they were close enough, built-in flamethrowers created a wall that even Valerie didn't want to test.

She pulled back toward the Pod, taking Robin with her. Garcia and Micky were still taking care of the force outside the hospital.

"What was that?" Robin asked, out of breath as they slid down next to the Pod.

Valerie just shook her head, trying to get a grasp on their situation.

"Welcome back, ladies!" Garcia said as he let off a couple rounds into the darkness.

A bullet hit the Pod, ricocheting off and pinging against the ground right next to Valerie's foot.

That gave her an idea.

"We're going to have to borrow the doors," she said, ripping one off as they looked at her in confusion. "Robin?"

Robin nodded, grabbed the other door, and heaved it off. "I hope this'll work."

"Hey, no complaining unless you have a better idea."

"What're *we* gonna do?" Micky shouted.

"Improvise," Valerie answered, but when he just stared at her blankly she sighed and heaved the Pod onto its side. "There. Stay behind it and keep the enemies on that side, or dead."

"We'll aim for keeping 'em dead."

She nodded, then led the charge back to the hospital fortress.

"We can still consider crawling through the sewers," Robin offered.

Valerie shook her head. "Not a chance."

The bullets were like a barrage of hail thudding against the doors. Mostly the doors held up, but a few times bullets tore through the metal, reminding Valerie to tell someone back in New York it was time for upgrades. By the time they reached the flamethrowers the shatterproof glass was looking like a spiderweb.

"Just go for it!" Valerie shouted, and charged.

Flames licked at her legs and she could feel them burn, but, as fast as they were running, the flames couldn't catch. A moment later she slammed the Pod door into the front door that, even though it was apparently barricaded, gave under her strength.

Her door was toast now, but Robin hadn't used *hers* as a battering ram, so she quickly took a stance in front of Valerie as a man with an old-style rifle began firing three-round bursts. Two others were still prepping a SAW, not believing they could've gotten in here so fast. But before they could unleash their hell-storm of bullets Robin tossed the door to take out the man with the rifle and Valerie threw herself up the wall, kicked off it, and landed on the upper level with the two machine gunners.

They gave her terrified looks before turning to run, but didn't make it more than three paces.

She took the first down with her sword, but held the second one out to Robin.

"Need a boost?"

Robin turned, debating, but finally nodded and sank her teeth in, moaning as the warm blood filled her mouth. She dropped him when she was done and wiped the blood off her chin with her sleeve.

"Who knows how much trouble we'll face in here," Robin noted defensively. "Might as well be ready."

Valerie nodded, but stood still. "Someday we'll find a way for you to not need it. To be like…"

"What, like you?" Robin smiled. "I'd take it in a heartbeat."

Valerie adjusted her grip on her sword and considered the two halls the stairs led to.

"Always go left," Robin stated. "Most people choose right, so I try to do the opposite as often as possible."

"Until everyone else figures out your trick."

"Impossible. Most people either don't care or are too stupid."

Valerie laughed. "Good attitude to have."

"Want to go in there and do our thing, or stay here chatting with me?"

With a shake of her head, Valerie led the way.

In the first room they found men and women strapping on protective gear, their weapons nearby as they readied themselves for the defense of the building.

"Too late," Valerie hissed as she fell upon them like Death herself.

Robin finished the last of them off and they moved to the next room, and from that to the next. By the time they were about seven rooms in the enemies coming at them were geared up and ready, but they were still no match for these two.

At least they weren't until they reached what looked like an old operating room where three Forsaken knelt behind an overturned metal table and opened fire on them. They dodged, but these ones were good shots and when the ladies flung themselves backward they found a roomful of Nosferatu—the mindless vampires. The Nosferatu attacked and the other vampires kept shooting, using the distraction to their advantage.

Two bullets took Valerie in the back and one hit Robin in the arm. Grunting in pain, teeth clenched, Valerie grabbed Robin and pulled her through an opening between some of their legs, leaving the Nosferatu to take the next shots.

The two ducked through metal doors into a corridor and ran, looking for a spot to lie low long enough for their bodies to at least heal partially. The sounds of pursuit came from behind, so Valerie tried the closest door. It didn't budge.

Robin looked around desperately, then pointed and said, "There!"

She led them to a counter, which the two jumped over.

"What's the plan here?" Valerie asked, noting that Robin had unslung her rifle.

"We don't often sit back and shoot our pursuers, but since my arm hurts like shit and your back has two red eyes staring at me every time you turn around, I think it's time."

Valerie couldn't argue that, but when she tried to unsling her own rifle the bullet wounds hurt like hell.

"I don't suppose you could…"

Robin grunted and grabbed the strap, simply cutting it instead of trying to unsling it. Handing it over, she nodded, then took aim at the doors.

A second later they burst open and Nosferatu streamed in. Bullets kept them at bay until the rifles got low on ammo, and by then the pile of Nosferatu was fairly large. It wouldn't keep them away for long, but for now it'd work.

"This doesn't feel right," Robin voiced the concern Valerie had been having this whole time. "If they're here, why all this? Wouldn't they be at risk too?"

"Maybe they're a couple floors up?"

"Or maybe they set us up." Robin emptied her clip, reached for another, and found she had no more. Narrowing her eyes at the doorway, she asked, "How well do you actually know Micky?"

That wasn't a bad question actually, but Valerie shook her head. "Diego, Cammie, the others…they vouch for him."

"After knowing him for many years, I'm sure." Robin gave her a doubtful stare.

"No way. I'll prove to you this wasn't a betrayal." She stretched, glad to feel the pain at least starting to subside. "You coming?"

"We aren't healed yet."

"And I won't wait that long." She started walking, pulling her hip pistol to shoot through the door as one of the Forsaken showed his face. The shot hit him between the eyes and he fell back.

Valerie ran through the halls, up more stairs, and through more corridors shouting for Lady Woo.

"Show yourself," she said, and each time she said it her heart filled with that much more doubt. Finally she just stopped. "I won't accept it!"

Robin pulled her around. "Two things. The longer you take to accept it, the more danger others could be in."

"And the second?"

"Do you smell—"

"Gas..." Valerie finished the question, processing it as she spoke.

"*The window!*" Robin shouted, and pulled Valerie with her. They dove out of the hallway into the closest room, and threw open the curtains to find that, in their haste, they had forgotten about the bars on the windows.

Valerie spun, looking for an option, and was about ready to try kicking out the bars when a young man entered the room. He had a receding hairline, black hair, and narrow eyes that seemed to be in an eternal frown.

"So, you two made it."

Valerie and Robin shared a look of confusion, then turned back to him.

"I'd hoped you would, or rather, my mother did." He smiled, hand on the room's light switch. "You see, I told her... I fucking *told* her I could do one last useful thing in this life."

"And what would that be?" Valerie asked. "Because if you think you have a chance here, you don't."

He laughed, shaking his head. "But don't you see? It's already over. For me it's been over for some time—nothing they can do once they find the lumps. But for you? You were dead the moment you became the monsters you are."

"We're not monster—"

Valerie's words were cut short by the man flipping the switch as he closed his eyes, a wide smile on his face. Instant explosions rocked the building, including a ball of flame bursting from the walls to fill the room. With vampire speed Valerie grabbed Robin and ran for the barred windows, throwing herself at them with such power that they gave. They fell to the ground below, Valerie clutching Robin to her front as she positioned herself to absorb the impact.

She landed on the same shoulder that had taken the impact on the bars above, and a piercing pain filled her as the shoulder bones cracked.

"Ahhh!" Valerie screamed, still rolling, then stopped to kneel and rock back and forth at the pain.

Robin went to her side and tried to help her to stand.

"I can't," Valerie shouted, holding her shoulder and turning back to watch the flames shooting out of the windows above.

"Val, we have to! If Micky was behind this, what about Garcia?"

The pain was certainly still there, but for a moment it was pushed aside by a sudden fear for their friend. He had come to the city to help them, and for all they knew they had left him surrounded by enemies with a betrayer at his back.

Coursing pain threatened to dull Valerie's senses as she stood, but she managed, her body still healing from the bullet wounds and now repairing a broken shoulder. They ran in the direction of the Pod, but as they rounded the building there was a new explosion overhead, then another that sent a chunk of the building flying out to nearly hit them.

It sounded like firecrackers going off in there, but Valerie knew it was likely explosives and munitions left to be caught in the fire and help finish her off in case the fire didn't.

Robin had fallen while dodging so Valerie helped her up with her good hand, and the two made it back to the front of the hospital. Before them the ground was covered in dead bodies, some human and some not.

When they glanced that way, the Pod was shaking. Finally it fell over, and they saw the reason: Garcia and Micky were struggling, fighting. As they watched, Garcia pinned Micky to the Pod. He landed a couple punches before the ladies reached them and then Valerie took over.

With her good hand she snatched Micky away from Garcia and demanded to know what happened.

"He wasn't actually shooting at them," Garcia said, nearly out of breath. "I noticed toward the end, then saw him about to turn on me."

JUSTIN SLOAN & MICHAEL ANDERLE

"And he led us here," Valerie added. "Which begs the question...why?"

Micky opened his mouth as if to argue, and but his eyes filled with tears. "Bullshit! I swear to God, or the gods!"

"Calm the hell down and tell us what's happening?" Valerie demanded, *pushing* fear into him. She took a deep breath, focusing so that she could tell if he was lying. "Were you behind this?"

"No. But Arturo...he's where I got most of my information. I hadn't thought about it. I mean, he was like a brother to me."

"That semi-brother nearly got you killed," Robin stated.

"I'm not buying it," Garcia countered. "You came at me."

Micky shook his head. "You and Arturo... I started piecing it together when the fire started. That he'd turned on me. I figured you and he... Maybe..."

"No," Valerie looked him dead in the eyes, "Garcia's legit. I trust him and the Colonel who sent him, so I'm not buying it. But if what you say about Arturo is true—"

"We have to get back." Garcia finished her sentence, face turning pale even in the darkness.

Valerie hung her head, trying not to think about what she might have done by rushing off like this, what damage might already have been caused because she trusted so easily. Everyone had always told her it was her weakness, and now it might've bitten her in the ass.

"I'm not accepting yet that Arturo is on the other side," she stated, slowly looking at each of them. "But I agree that there has been false intelligence given, and I admit that I acted rashly. I'm sorry."

"There's no need for that," Robin replied. "First we deal with the situation, then we worry about who was behind what."

Garcia nodded, still cautiously watching Micky. Valerie joined the sergeant in staring at him.

"You're not off the hook yet," Valerie said to the large man, although the energy coming from him told her that he was telling the truth. "I hope my trust in you was founded, but we'll talk some more after this. In the meantime, you're going to have to stay out of it."

"My friends and family are back there, possibly at risk of death, and you want me to stay out of it?" He tried to get up, to resist her strength, but after a moment he quit. The ferocity was still in his eyes, however. "Would you be able to do that?"

She licked her lips, shook her head, and frowned.

"Robin, what do I do here?"

"What?" Robin stared at her, baffled.

"I'm too trusting; I know that. Usually I think it's a part of me I should embrace, but I might be slowly learning that there're limits to that. I want you to tell me what to do here."

"You can't seriously be considering letting him fight," Garcia argued. "What if he was behind this?"

She breathed deeply and turned to him. "I told you I can read emotions, right? Almost like thoughts. We've directly asked him, and he denied it. When he said he didn't do what you thought he did, he was telling the truth. And he has a point. If I were to tell him not to fight and then someone he cared about was killed, that would be the same as me having killed that person, as I see it. I know you are suspicious, but you'll have to trust me on this one."

"I *was* shooting at them, Garcia. You have to believe me," Micky pleaded.

"Your aim just fucking sucks that bad?" Garcia demanded.

Micky cringed, then shrugged. "I'm not saying I was scared, but… When I'm under pressure, sometimes it does."

"Well, fuckity-fucksticks." Garcia kicked the Pod.

"Hey, careful with that," Valerie snapped. "We're going to need it to get back in time."

They looked from her to the Pod, doubtful.

"Will it make it that far?" Robin asked.

"Only one way to find out," Valerie replied with an ironic grin. "Faith."

"Also known as trust, in a sense." Robin chuckled. "Oh, boy."

Valerie cautiously released Micky, then turned to Garcia. "Are we good here? You boys going to play nice?"

Garcia considered the question, then nodded. "You say he's good, Val, I say you're good for it." He extended a hand to Micky. "Friends?"

Micky chuckled. "No fucking way. But two-guys-who-don't-like-each-other-a-whole-lot-right-now-but-can-fight-together-and-maybe-be-friends-again-someday?" He shook the hand. "Sure."

"I'll take it." Garcia ran a bloodied hand through his hair, not realizing that he was getting gore in his mane. "Damn, I almost killed you."

"And once again, Valerie saved the day." Micky chuckled as they all got into the Pod. "Let's hope it stays that way. Saving the day, I mean. Some people back there might need it."

"We left them in good hands," Valerie countered, glancing at him as she slid into the pilot's seat.

"Yes, but how many of those hands actually belong to other side?" Micky asked.

"Dammit." She made sure they were buckled in securely, considering that there were no doors, and then started to lift off. "And Fred?"

"Let's keep our fingers crossed for Fred," Garcia replied. "Right now we have to ensure New York is safe."

Valerie nodded, and began maneuvering the Pod toward the city. It didn't work perfectly, more than once faltering in its forward momentum, but overall they progressed in the right direction.

Fred could still show up with others at his side to join New York. It was possible. She hoped a whole army showed up with

Fred carrying Lady Woo's head on a platter, but doubted she'd be so lucky.

The only lucky things she could see right now were that the city had walls, and that Cammie, Royland, Davies, and some other smart and powerful people were there to keep it safe.

She hoped.

Just then a buzzing reminded her that the comm device had been left in the Pod. She ducked down, pain shooting through her shoulder as she picked it up. She cringed.

"Hello?"

"Val, thank goodness!" Sandra's voice came through, crackling. "Get back here. They're in the city!"

"We're on our way," Valerie said, and pushed the Pod for all she was worth as the comm device clicked off. "Sandra? Sandra!"

No response.

CHAPTER SEVENTEEN

Outside New York

Cammie was standing around with Royland and some of the new fighters in the ruins just outside New York, telling the story of how she had met Royland and about their first sparring match.

"And when I saw the way he moved, I knew I had to get him in the sack," she finished, giving him a loving look. She didn't understand why he rolled his eyes and blushed.

The fighters busted up laughing.

"We thought you were going to tell us about the first time you realized you loved him or something," one of the women at the back of the group called.

Cammie chuckled. "Ohhh, well, I mean, that wasn't nearly as eventful. If you all could've been there to see how he—"

"Okay, okay, that's enough." Royland had stood and was waving to everyone to keep their cool when he stared past them and said, "Oh, shit!"

He was looking at the city.

Cammie spun to follow his line of sight, and that was when the sound hit them. An explosion and a burst of light came from HQ, and then it started to fall—at least the top of it.

"How the..." Cammie started to ask, but was cut off by battle cries and gunfire from the hills.

She turned that way and saw the armies charging down at them. These weren't just the people who had scattered earlier; there were at least three times that many. And if she was seeing right, they had a line of wolves and even some tigers in the lead. She wouldn't be surprised if the fast-moving people right behind them were vampires, though there were fewer of them.

With a glance back at Royland she yelled, "Let's fucking do this!"

"You don't want to get behind the walls?"

"Honey, think 'WWBAD.' Bethany Anne wouldn't hide behind walls. She'd bitch-slap the hell out of these ass-munchers for daring to attack us. Am I right? Now pull yourself up by the balls and let's go!"

She charged, her two short blades in hand.

When Royland caught up to her he shouted, "We're going to have to do something about your foul mouth when you get excited, especially if you ever want to have a dog around the house. I don't want him learning to talk like that."

"First, everyone knows bitches are better. Second, I'm pretty sure dogs can't talk."

He shrugged and went into full-on killer mode.

For their part, most of the people who had switched sides remained loyal now. Some ran and others held back to look for cover among the ruins, but most moved forward toward the fight.

About halfway to the enemy Cammie noticed a shape in the distance moving their way, and for a moment wondered where the enemy had gotten a Pod. Then she saw Valerie hanging out, shooting her pistol at the enemy below.

Only, as the Pod drew closer, it became clear that it was beat to hell and had no doors. What had they been through?

Having spotted her, Valerie brought the Pod down and shoved

it over so that it could act as a barrier as their foe charged into the open. Royland took a spot behind it and started shooting, Micky and Garcia doing the same, but Valerie and Robin went straight for Cammie.

"What's happened?" Valerie asked.

"The explosion. HQ…" She pointed back. "I saw it go."

"Sandra called and said the enemy was in the city, but since then I haven't been able to get through."

"The water," Robin said.

"What?"

Robin just pointed, and both ladies turned to the south where a shape was visible moving on the water. Then another. And another.

"Those fuck-faced mold-eating barf-holes!" Cammie shouted. She glanced around, trying to figure out their next move.

Valerie'd had the same reaction, but she stopped, put a hand on Cammie's shoulder, and said, "Can you hold them off?"

"What? I mean, yes. *Hell yes!*"

"Do it. We need the outside of this city safe, and I'm leaving that up to you. Robin and I will clear it from within."

"We will?" Robin asked.

Valerie nodded. "Know how to swim?"

Robin blinked, then nodded. "Sure. Maybe."

"Time to learn."

And with that they were off, moving toward the water in the distance. Royland turned back, eyes wide.

"Where the fuck are they going?"

"Didn't you say something about watching mouths?" Cammie replied, checking the enemy, who were almost upon them. "Those two will take care of whatever caused that explosion while we deal with this rat problem."

"So we get to be the exterminators," he said, turning to unload several rounds before rotating back as some more came his way. With a glance at the sky, he added, "We better make it quick."

She frowned, then looked up and saw what he meant. While it wasn't quite sunrise yet, the stars were fading and the darkness was turning to a silvery blue at the edge of the sky.

"If it comes to it, get out of here while you can," she told him. "If you're back there in a house, you're the best kind of insurgent should they overrun us. Out here in the sun you're just dead."

He nodded and she cursed herself for not insisting he bring the sun suit. Oh, well, now wasn't the time for second guesses—it was the time for killing.

"Watch this," she said with a chuckle, then ran and, using the Pod to vault, went high in the air to land right on top of the line of vampires, tearing into them with her blades. The lead Weres turned back to take her on, exposing their backs to Royland who followed her lead.

Now they're in trouble, she thought as her dance began. All around them the other fighters surged forward, and what had been two sides exchanging gunfire moments before suddenly became the biggest brawl Cammie had ever been in. If she hadn't been worried about the people she loved, she would've been having a blast.

"Behind you!" Royland shouted, and she turned to see a tiger leaping at her. Its claws took her across the face, but she spun with it and plunged both blades into its torso, pulling it open like a sack of toys. Gross, bloody toys.

A vampire had gone for Royland but he ducked the strike and came up behind it, snapping its neck before kicking the body away from him. He held onto the head, twisting again as the body fell so that the head and body tore apart.

It was sick, and yet…very hot.

Cammie went for a vampire then, but had to divert her attention toward a wolf that had started tearing into someone's shoulder. She cut through it, but was tackled by its friend and her swords went flying.

Guess that means it's transformation time, she thought, and became the large wolf, embracing her inner beast. With a growl she went at them, tearing and clawing and overall having a grand ol' time.

———

Espinoza took another shot at the enemy below, but it was getting harder with all the hand-to-hand fighting down there. He glanced at his boys—they were just as restless as he felt—and then stowed the sniper rifle.

"You know, forget this," he said, waving them to follow. "Grab one of those arc batons they showed us, a baseball bat, or whatever the hell your weapon of choice is. We're not letting Cammie and Royland kill them all while we just sit here looking pretty."

"Fuckin' A," Okeland said, fixing a knife onto the end of his rifle as they started walking.

"That's your weapon of choice?" Espinoza asked.

Okeland smiled, showing off his front gold teeth. "You know it. I'm going back to the old days here, boss."

"As long as it makes them dead, I'm all for it."

He preferred batons personally, and took two. Others had already run out to join the fight, so the gate was open and they were able to move out easily enough. With a glance back, he saw Arturo lingering at the wall, looking out at the water.

"Arturo, you in on this?" he asked.

The man shook his head. "I feel compelled to keep the city safe, but I'll cover you from up here."

Espinoza frowned. *To each his own.*

He led them to the tipped pod where he had seen Garcia land. Best to join up with the only other FDG soldier here, he figured. They all charged, soon finding enemies trying to tackle, stab, and shoot them from all directions.

He was starting to wonder if coming out here had been a mistake when Garcia came up from his left, slamming the butt-end of his rifle into a forehead, then turning to kick another one back, where he got plowed through by someone else's attack.

"Arturo," Garcia shouted as he dodged a rock and then moved for cover behind the Pod, even though it was mostly surrounded now. "You seen him?"

"He's back at the gate. What's up?"

Garcia cursed and was about to answer when an attacker got him with a metal rod right across the head.

Micky was there a moment later, lifting his buddy from the ground and pulling him away from the chaos as much as possible, while Espinoza fought to keep the closest enemies back.

"He was asking about your buddy Arturo?" Espinoza asked, pulling out his pistol to shoot two down.

"That's right. We think he might've betrayed us. He's with the other side."

"Bullshit! I saw him…" He thought about it as he fought. What had he really seen of Arturo, other than someone who liked to shoot people. To kill. Even when he was killing an enemy, Espinoza felt wrong about it. Even if he did enjoy it in some weird way, he still felt bad about feeling good.

But not Arturo, he had noticed.

"Shit, he's back there." Espinoza motioned to the gate.

Micky nodded. "I'll take care of him." He slung Garcia over his shoulders and took off toward the gate.

"Need any help?" Espinoza called.

"Nah, you just take care of these other sons of bitches. I'll deal with that one."

Espinoza got back into the fight out of necessity because he saw a woman with a scythe running for Okeland. He lifted the pistol and aimed and the first shot hit her in the ear, but then his gun was empty. The shot had been enough to distract her at least, so he pulled out the two batons and charged into the fray.

He was in his element. One he wanted to avoid as much as possible, but when he was in it? Damn, it felt good.

While the battle raged behind them, Valerie and Robin reached the edge of the water. A glance to their left caught her by surprise, because somehow there was a large head and two eyes staring at her—the head of the Statue of Liberty. She remembered seeing the headless body when she had first arrived, and had wondered.

Judging by the discoloration and barnacles, it had ended up in the water, but been recovered at some point.

"Whoa," Robin said, and it almost made Valerie laugh. That one exclamation reminded her how young the woman really was.

Past the head there was a bit of a walkway they could use to reach the point where the small flat boats were docking. Two were already there, and three more were on the way.

"Looks like we won't be swimming after all," Valerie said with relief.

"We have a plan?"

Valerie nodded. "Girl, I've always got a plan. It just usually involves the following three-step approach: run over, kick some ass, and then kick some more.

"I've noticed."

Valerie started to take a step toward the boats, but Robin held out a hand.

"You have a better plan, I'm guessing." Valerie folded her arms, waiting. "Out with it, then."

"I like your plan, don't get me wrong, but what if one of us joins the crews that landed while the other stays behind to put a stop to the rest of them. That way the first person—I'm guessing you—moves with this group to connect with whoever they already have in the city, and gets rid of them."

"It would save us from having to run around looking for them," Valerie admitted.

"Trust me. I can handle the docks, you take care of your

friends."

Valerie nodded. "Deal, dammit. But once it's over, join me at the wall to finish the fight out there. I want to preserve as many lives as possible."

"Roger that, Chief."

"Don't call me that."

They ran forward in a crouch, careful to avoid being seen. The night breeze was colder than usual, carrying with it the stench of death. Or maybe that was just in her head. Either way, she found herself scrunching her nose and trying to keep her footsteps light.

How odd, she thought, *that I have never come out to this side of the city before.* It looked different from here; taller and grander, except for the top of HQ where the fire was raging. It was only somewhat visible between two buildings from this angle, but it reflected on the clouds above.

As they approached the nearest boat, they saw that the three people emerging had their attention on the fire too.

Robin took out the closest and Valerie dropped the woman who was next in line. The third turned with wide eyes, mouth opening to sound the alarm, so Valerie leaped and crushed his larynx with a fist.

"Ouch," Robin whispered as she watched him gagging, trying to catch his breath, and then falling back into the boat. They hastily followed him onto the boat to get out of sight.

Valerie quickly went through the crews' belongings, dressing herself as they had. She even attached a weird sort of breastplate and shoulder guard like the guy had been wearing, figuring it could be useful for the fight to come. Although her shoulder was already starting to mend, she didn't want to risk it getting hurt again so soon after breaking it.

"These people are straight out of the days that were considered old even before the Great Collapse," Valerie said, quickly fastening the armor. "How do I look?"

"Ancient."

"*Watch it!*"

Robin smirked. "And you hurry up. Catch up to that last group."

"You'll be fine?"

"I'll linger in this boat, and when the next one comes in, play vampire at the water's edge." Robin smiled, her pointed teeth showing. "I'm even looking forward to it. I mean, I learned all that assassin stuff, but mostly we just charge straight into situations."

Valerie shook her head with a smile. "You'll do amazing. Wish me luck."

"Luck." They hugged, and for a moment Valerie wondered, but by then Robin was pulling back. She smiled expectantly.

"Right." Valerie nodded, then turned and went on her way.

She found the other group not too far ahead, sneaking through the city although they were armed. They didn't even notice she was there at first, but when one of them turned and saw her he motioned to her to hurry up. Now that she thought about it, she didn't look so different from the woman back there on the boat.

This could work, if her goal was to stay concealed. But that was a very short-term goal.

Loud shouting came from ahead, then a group of armed men ran past. Valerie's new friends stayed hidden before darting across, pointing to a building opposite HQ.

The same building she had met Jackson in so long ago.

Now that she knew where they were going, she didn't have any more use for them. With a silent bound she took out the rear one, dropping him by slashing her claws into his neck.

The other four kept moving forward, weapons held at the ready for anything that might come from up ahead. Little did they know that "anything" was behind them.

A shot was fired nearby and the one in the lead dropped. The others had started to run when a group of men came out and attacked. Valerie took a step back and one of the men turned his rifle on her, then froze.

"Jackson?"

He looked baffled and stayed put, and the man to his left turned on him to attack. Valerie was there in a split second to ensure it didn't happen.

"Thanks," Jackson hissed as the man fell, and the others moved over to see what was happening.

"Val," Davies said, "what the hell are you wearing?"

"I'm undercover," she replied. "We saw them coming off the water. Robin's there, but you might want to send some vampires to help her out. HQ secured yet?"

"We think so," Davies replied. "A couple of our men were injured, but the only ones dead—get this!—are the prisoners."

"Damn. I sure hope they weren't wrongfully accused then." She took a breath and realized the healing had done its job on her. Good timing. "Listen, get more people on the walls. I've got this taken care of."

"We don't know where they hit us from or where they could be. Or if there're more of them."

"These people just arrived, so unless you already killed them?" Jackson shook his head.

"Then I know where they'll be. I got this." She started to leave, then paused, hand on Jackson's arm. "Wait. Sandra…is she safe?"

He nodded. "We have a team protecting the entrance to their hideout. She dropped the comm device when she was running to get back down there. We'll find it, but haven't had time yet. I know she was worried."

"Thank you. I'll have a chance to see her myself soon enough."

They moved on, splitting up so some could go to the docks and others to secure HQ. Valerie headed for the building she had seen the invaders motioning to.

CHAPTER EIGHTEEN

New York

Valerie snuck into the building, doing her best to appear as if she were one of the invaders and this was the plan.

Oddly, the building was exactly as she remembered it. There was still a hole where she had smashed someone's head once through the wall long ago. Or was this a hole one of her friends had created by smashing someone's head through it? She couldn't quite remember, but felt a sense of nostalgia come over her all the same.

As she walked through the hall she touched the rough drywall with her fingertips, wondering what and who she would find here.

"Where are the others?" a voice hissed, and she turned to see a woman with a rifle. Where the woman was standing she might have appeared intimidating, hiding in the shadows. Not so with Valerie.

"They were all taken down on the way over," Valerie replied, doing her best to sound shaken and worried. "But I'm here."

"Get upstairs," the woman replied, disgust heavy in her voice.

"We're getting ready to make our next move. Dammit, if you hadn't lost the others…"

"I'll try to keep more alive next time."

It seemed like the woman was going to say something else, but then she just clucked her tongue and made a shooing motion.

Valerie sneered, making her way up the narrow stairs. Anticipation building, she waited at the last stair at the top.

"Kill him then, to teach his traitor father a lesson," a woman's voice said, muffled. That didn't sound good, so Valerie *pushed* fear and stepped into the room.

Everyone turned to her at once, and to her surprise there were already approximately twenty individuals gathered.

"Who are you, girl?" a woman at the center asked. The woman looked very similar to the young man from the hospital, and Valerie knew it had to be none other than Lady Woo. so

"Who am I?" Valerie stepped forward, *pushing* harder with fear this time, so hard that those on the outside of the group stepped back. A trickle of piss hit the floor and a puddle formed at one man's feet.

"What the hell is going on?" another shouted, confused.

"Keep your voices down, dammit!" Lady Woo commanded, then looked at Valerie skeptically. Her eyes widened. "It's you, isn't it? The one they all talk so much about."

Valerie was about to answer but froze as she saw who they had been talking about killing—the boy, Fred's son. She couldn't quite remember his name, but it was something similar to Fred—she knew that much.

She raised her eyes to see who was holding the back of his shirt. *Arturo!*

Valerie growled, revealing her sharp vampire teeth. Her eyes glowed red, and she saw the matching glow of red from the closer people.

"Kill this bitch," Lady Woo commanded, trying to sound much

tougher than the break in her voice halfway through the sentence would indicate.

"Sorry, but...can't let that happen," Valerie replied, and then charged. These people had managed to sneak in through the backdoor of their city while the front was under attack and blow up the building Valerie had once considered home. It wasn't totally gone, but it wasn't all there either. And they would've tried to kill Sandra and the others, so it gave Valerie no grief to take their lives.

She went for Arturo first, but he pulled back, knife to the boy's throat and shouted, "Stay back!" She cursed, changing direction to deal with the others instead. She was fairly certain that Arturo understood the implied contract here—if he harmed the boy, he would die.

Weapons emerged quickly and fell to the ground almost as fast, followed by their owner's corpses.

Valerie worked in an inward spiral so that by the time she only had Lady Woo and a few others left—the few others likely being the other leaders—they were surrounded by a circle of the dead. *Almost poetic*, Valerie thought as she wiped her bloodied claws on her pants. She glanced at Arturo, cautious, debating whether she was fast enough to reach him before he could plunge that knife into the boy's neck.

"So what exactly was the plan here?" Valerie asked. "Sic your cancerous son on us instead of spending the last days with him? Not good." She killed one more of them with a simple slash across the throat. "Then attack our city, burn it to the ground, and create an empire by killing anyone you saw as an inconvenience...even children. Did I get any of that wrong?"

"We work for the greater good," a tall older man to Lady Woo's right began. "We formed the Indie Network to—"

He was cut off—literally. His head rolled, landing next to Lady Woo. She kicked it away, drawing two pistols and turning on Valerie. The remaining two men did the same, although one had a rifle, so she dove through the middle of them and came up swinging. One turned, spraying the other with bullets, and she ended the last man.

Lady Woo shot at her again, but Valerie ducked. One shot tore through the air inches from her head and the other dinged off her shoulder armor.

"Here's the thing, lady," Valerie said, standing tall and refusing to give this woman any of the power she had hurt so many people to obtain. "In this city we don't cower to tyrants. In this city we fight for each other out of love. And when we kill, we kill only those who have tried to take this from us, and then we kill without mercy."

Valerie glanced back at Arturo and the boy, and Lady Woo noticed. Dammit, *she noticed!* A smile played on her lips.

"Arturo," she started, "if this vampire piece of shit so much as makes a move for either of us, kill that boy. Got it?"

"Loud and clear," Arturo replied.

Valerie breathed deeply, hating this. She weighed her options, torn. "What'd she promise you, Arturo? You get to be a leader now, is that it?" She gestured to the dead on the floor. "Plenty of openings, aren't there?"

He glared, and that was enough of an answer.

"I hope it was worth your life," she said, her muscles twitching. *She would have to go for it.*

"Don't you dare," he shouted, suddenly terrified. He backed up, the knife starting to draw blood, and the boy whimpered, his wide eyes pleading with Valerie. "Don't you *dare!*"

Another presence caught Valerie's attention. She sniffed—it was familiar. But where, and why now? Another traitor? The newcomer's aura hit her and it was clearly aggression, though not directed at her.

With a crash, Micky came through the wall right behind Arturo, knocking the blade free and wrestling him away from the boy in one quick movement. As the blade clattered away and the

JUSTIN SLOAN & MICHAEL ANDERLE

boy fell to his knees, Lady Woo reached for a gun, but Valerie acted first.

She sprang forward, throwing Lady Woo into the far wall. The woman looked stunned at first, but as she recovered and stood, that turned into anger.

"You can't kill me. You need me!" she shouted. "How else will you keep my people in check? They won't listen to—"

"*ENOUGH!*" Valerie was a hundred percent certain in that instant that this was not someone she could allow to live. She leaped forward, pulling the woman's head back by the hair, and sank her teeth into her neck. Not because she needed the blood, but because she wanted to feel the life drain from this one slowly.

When it was done she let the corpse drop to the floor, wiped her mouth, and spat.

New York was theirs once again.

Valerie turned just in time to see Micky plunge Arturo's own blade into the man's throat.

"That's for betraying your own people," Micky said, then fell beside the dying man, eyes wide and glinting with tears.

"Micky, take the boy to Sandra. We'll reunite him with his father in the morning."

Pulling himself together, Micky nodded.

"Come on, Eddie Jr.," he said. "I've got you."

That was the name! She smiled, nodded to them, and took off.

Valerie ran back to the water, where she found four more boats covered in blood. Shots were still being fired outside the wall, but nothing this way. Nothing more had happened in the city since she had dealt with Lady Woo and the others.

"Robin?" she hissed as she reached the dock.

A figure appeared at her side and she nearly had a heart attack, but smiled at the sight of Robin's victorious stance.

"I think we got 'em all."

"And the men I sent over?" Robin gestured and Valerie saw them along the wall, weapons at the ready.

"We figured it made sense in case any got through."

"Good thinking." Valerie beamed, looking at the sunrise coming over the water. The sky was already that light yellow—almost gold—it got just before the sun poked up, and that meant Robin needed to get inside. "Find Sandra and tell her I'll be there soon. I need to make sure Royland's off the battlefield. The rest of you, come with me."

"I will, and I'll check on my parents. They went underground too, right? Same place?"

Valerie nodded. "I'll see you tonight. Get some rest."

They agreed and Robin ran off at full speed. She had clearly been too focused on the task to consider the situation with the sunlight—a nearly fatal lack of focus.

"I'm going to move faster than you can," Valerie told the men. "Just do what you can when you get there."

Running ahead of them and not worried about stealth now, Valerie reached the battlefield and was pleasantly surprised. The people with their backs to New York were largely still alive, firing on random stragglers from the enemy army. They had a group of the enemy pinned down; some shooters who were using a mound of corpses as cover.

This will take a long time to clean up, she thought. She found Royland and Cammie at the edge of the battlefield, Cammie already urging him to go.

"Why aren't you in shelter yet?" Valerie demanded.

Royland glanced back, glared, and asked. "Did we win? Lady Woo?"

"I drank her blood and felt her life drain away. Happy?"

He closed his eyes, smiled, and said, "Yes."

"Then get the fuck out of here!" Cammie shouted.

After kissing her briefly, he ran for cover. Valerie turned to

165

assess the situation. On the left was another force that was firing occasionally at the one surviving group. Valerie strained her eyes to see, but was pretty sure that was Fred over there.

"They arrived not long ago," Cammie announced, beaming. "At first we were worried and about to attack, but they saw who was who and made it clear they were on our side when they started lobbing grenades at the enemy. Oh, and they," Cammie pointed to another group on the far side, "came with this guy…called himself Gerald and said you knew him? Vampire type."

Valerie laughed. "No way. He's in the city now?"

She smiled, glad he had shown up. That would be a fun reunion.

Valerie gave Fred a wave, then turned back to her friend, hands on her hips.

"Want to end this like we used to?" Valerie asked once he was gone.

"Girl power?" Cammie asked. "Let's do it."

"I was thinking more like a 'Ladies' Night Out' kinda thing, but yeah."

"Less talking, more killing." Cammie transformed and together they ran out to deal with the last of the enemy.

It was over as quickly as it had begun, the two ladies tearing the enemy fighters apart before they even had a chance to scream. By the time they finished the sun shone over New York city, glinting off buildings and casting shadows on the dead. Valerie stood at the edge of the city looking at her new army, this motley crew of fresh New York citizens.

"You have all earned your place here among us," she shouted, her voice carrying loud and clear. "Remember that the days of violence are behind us, however. We will accept trainees into the military and the police, since we must have both. There will always be some who try to act out, to cause pain and suffering. But we will be the rising sun that casts aside such darkness. We will stand as one and say, 'Not in *our* city. Not on *our* Earth.' Will you all agree to that?"

Cheers rose from the crowd; she had them.

"Come on, then…let us welcome you to your new home. Get some rest, because as you can see, we have a lot of cleanup to do."

The cheers faltered somewhat there, but as they started moving for the city the smiles were plenty wide.

Before she started to follow them, she saw Espinoza and his men heading her way.

"Thank you, soldiers. We wouldn't have made it back here last night without your help. And I'm sure you did your part to see us through until morning too."

Espinoza stuck out his hand and she shook it.

"Any time you all want to come visit us," he said, "we'll be around. Just give the Colonel a call on that comm device. I'd love to sit down and have that beer with you."

"Me too. Aren't you staying?"

He glanced around at his men. "We'll rest up, but then we gotta get back. It's a long journey, and I'm anxious to make sure our Pod is where I left it."

She laughed. "Tell you what. While you rest, I'll run out there and bring it back, if that works for you. So it's all ready in the morning."

He nodded. "You truly go above and beyond, Val. We all consider ourselves lucky to have had the chance to fight by your side."

His men agreed, and they all followed her into the city to bunk down for the night. It was a good thing she had met the Colonel when she did, or these guys and the comm devices wouldn't have been possible. Without the comm device she might not have made it back from Europe at all, and tonight she wouldn't have returned in time to deal with the invaders who had entered the city.

She owed much more than her life to that man and his team.

CHAPTER NINETEEN

New York

Sandra heard someone entering and ran to the door. When she saw the guards—Diego among them—moving aside, she knew it was a good sign. Even better when she noticed that the sounds of shooting had ceased.

"Who is it?" came whispers from behind her.

Then an older couple came forward, and one proclaimed, "Robin!" and in came that very person, running to their arms despite the blood still caked on her. It was clear that she had tried to wipe it off, but she hadn't done a good enough job. When she pulled back, some was on the parents.

They would have to find some good showers, but not until they'd rested. Everyone here needed a break, since sleeping during the battle hadn't been realistic.

Robin smiled at the sight of Sandra, and moved toward her to give her a hug, but Sandra held up her hands and said, "Maybe when you're cleaned up." At the frown, Sandra said, "Screw it!" and pulled Robin in.

"Wow, it's really growing, huh?" Robin looked at Sandra's belly. "How much longer?"

"Several months still," Sandra replied, shaking her head. "I hope the baby's safe after all the stress of tonight."

"I'm sure she is," Robin replied, and then yawned.

"Come on, daughter," her father said, taking her by the arm. "We have a bed for you."

"Actually," Sandra interjected, "now that the fighting is over, we have more comfortable quarters above to retire to if you'd prefer."

"Thank you," Robin's mom replied, "but honestly, we're so wiped we'll barely be able to make it to the cots in here before passing out."

Sandra laughed and nodded. "I get that. But...Robin?"

"Uh, right," Robin turned back. "Sorry, so tired I nearly forgot. Valerie's safe, she took out the indie leaders, and the war is completely over. It's all...good." Another yawn.

"Thanks. Now go get some sleep."

"No argument there."

Robin walked off, one arm in each of her parents'.

Sandra turned back to Diego, who had come up behind her and wrapped her in his arms.

"You hear that, dear?" he asked. "We have a full day of rest and relaxation ahead of us."

"Are you kidding?" She scoffed. "I can get maybe a couple of hours sleep, then we need to get the café open. Get this city moving again. The people need to know we're doing business as usual."

He laughed, kissed her, and rested his head against hers as his hand caressed her belly. "I love you. Both of you."

"We love you too," she said, and then, when her head swam, she wrapped her arms around him. "Help me find a bed, please?"

"With pleasure." He picked her up in both arms and, careful not to bang her head against the door frame, carried her outside.

"You can't lug me all the way home, Diego—come on! A cot will do."

"Not for *my* lady it won't. And just watch me."

She smiled dreamily and laid her head against his chest. As his heartbeat lulled her to sleep, all she could think about was how perfectly happy she was.

When Valerie finally stumbled into the underground hideout, she was led to where Robin had passed out beside her parents.

She stood there for a moment just smiling and looking at them, thinking how nice it must be to have parents who loved you and cared for you. Maybe her parents were out there somewhere, still thinking of her and loving her even if they thought she was dead. If they were still alive they would likely be quite old, she realized. Close to death's door themselves.

Maybe it would have been nice to search the world for them. She would have liked that, but knew how unrealistic that would be. Moreover, she had a mission, and she would have to make certain sacrifices to see that mission through.

After all, she had been appointed by Michael himself. She was his Justice Enforcer, and would see that title through to the end—or until his return.

EPILOGUE

New York

Clouds billowed over the city state of New York. Lightning flashed and thunder rumbled as chaotically as ever, but that was the only form of chaos the people of New York had seen for months. The final victory had sealed it once and for all. Peace had settled over the land, formed through blood and friendship, ties set in stone with the FDG to the west and others throughout America and Canada since.

Garcia had, after insisting on a couple beers and one more chocolate croissant, taken off back west with the other FDG men, though Valerie had been sad to see him go. These last few months had been much lonelier without him.

She got it though—why TH would want him at his side. She was sure the Colonel had big plans for Garcia.

Valerie watched the storms above with a smile and the knowledge that they meant nothing more than a coming rain. They weren't symbolic; they just *were*.

It was an odd sensation, or had been at first. *Peace*.

Many of the men and women who had switched sides had stayed, setting up south of the city; outside, actually. The New

Yorkers had helped them rebuild the ruined area so they could expand the city. Some were even moving across the river. Others had returned to their home areas with promises to form a new network, one of peace and friendship. If it didn't stick, at least now they knew what they would be up against.

She had a good feeling about the peace lasting, especially since she had used her limited mindreading ability to see how truthful the people were before letting them leave. Had there been disagreements or the occasional crazy person starting violence? A thief or two in Capital Square? Of course. That couldn't be avoided, but the city was doing its best to make a difference. She glanced over at HQ, now mostly rebuilt and housing the police. Across town by the park, the barracks was still in operation and New York's soldiers still trained.

What role would Valerie play in a world where peace was the norm? How would she use her power, her skills in battle, when all the world required of her was friendship?

At least she had that, and one aspect of that friendship kept her going: anticipation. Sandra's baby was due any day now.

So it was that when Valerie's comm device buzzed and she saw Diego's name she answered, her voice cracking with excitement.

"It's time!" Diego nearly screamed. "The baby's coming!"

Valerie wasn't sure she had ever moved so fast in any of her battles or life-and-death struggles. She darted through her door, hopped to the nearest rooftop, and bounded across the tops of nearby buildings to reach the one near the city center that had been set up as New York's hospital. It was about time they had a real medical facility, and it had made sense to move it outside the former Enforcer HQ now that the city had moved away from its military stance.

In the months following their victory over the indie network some people had begun training in medical services, others in the arts, and many were pursuing hobbies that could only found in times of peace. It was like the world of old, Valerie imagined—or as close as it would ever be.

And now Sandra was in that hospital, about to give birth to an actual human! The thought still amazed Valerie.

She reached the edge of Capital Square and worked her way down the fire escapes, jumping the last bit and rolling with it; not caring how much the fall hurt. She healed in a matter of seconds and kept sprinting toward the hospital. When she reached the doors she burst through, a blur until she reached the front desk where she stopped, realizing she didn't know what room Sandra was in.

She was about to ask when Felix appeared from a side hallway with a man on his arm.

"Over here!" Felix shouted, smiling widely at the sight of her. "They kicked us out, but—"

"They'll have a damn hard time doing that to me," she replied, jogging over and giving Felix a hug, glad to see him back and at it again despite the wound he had taken a few months back.

"Hurry up then, or you'll miss it," he said, and watched her with his arm around his boyfriend—one of the men with the devil patch on his leather jacket. *They are a good match*, Valerie thought as she turned, ducking into the room he had motioned her toward.

The sight of Sandra spread-legged caught her off-guard, but she quickly moved to her side opposite Diego. "Didn't miss it yet, did I?"

Sandra glared, but Diego chuckled as the doctor entered.

"They say she's fully dilated," Diego replied.

"Too much detail," Valerie replied. "Just…get that baby out so I can meet it already."

"It's not an *it!*" Sandra grunted with a glare as the doctor prepared her.

"Okay, count of three," the doctor said. "We'll try this again. Ready?"

JUSTIN SLOAN & MICHAEL ANDERLE

"A few false starts," Diego explained, then yelped as Sandra squeezed his hand extra hard. Good thing he was a Were and would heal, because her fingernails had drawn blood.

The next few minutes were a blur to Valerie, who, despite all the pain and suffering she had endured, couldn't fathom how Sandra was doing this. It was an alien experience, something she imagined she was closer to Diego in understanding than Sandra. She stood there holding her best friend's hand and encouraging her through it all, and then in a burst of yuck and joy the baby was in the doctor's arms and Sandra was crying.

Everything went blurry and for a moment Valerie wondered if something was wrong, then she realized that she was crying too.

"It's a girl," the doctor proclaimed, cutting the umbilical cord and quickly wiping the baby clean before gently placing her on Sandra's exposed chest. For a moment the baby's eyes seemed to look around and then she reached for the nipple, latching on a moment later.

"That's the fastest I've seen a baby do that," the doctor said with a pleasant smile, and then excused herself.

Valerie lingered a moment, amazed the beautiful sight of this weird-looking tiny baby, then kissed Sandra on the forehead and said, "Congratulations, she's amazing," before excusing herself too and making for the door.

She wanted to give them space, but also wanted to hide the tears she knew would return any minute—even if they were of joy. Being exposed like that wasn't in her bag of normalness. As she reached the door, Diego called out to her.

"Val, wait!"

She turned, a tilt to her head as she continued to struggle to keep the tears back.

"We want to tell you while we're still awake…" He bit his lip, smiling at Sandra. "It was thirty hours of labor, after all. Do you want to tell her, dear?"

Sandra, hand on the back of her newborn as she sucked, working to get her first meal, smiled and said, "Her name. If it was a girl, we both agreed—"

"Don't you say it," Valerie warned, already knowing what was coming as her vision blurred again.

"Her name's Valerie," Sandra finished, biting her lip and then smiling. "Valerie, meet *baby* Valerie."

That was it—the tears couldn't be stopped now. She wiped her eyes, smiled, and said, "Thank you," then turned and went out to the waiting area where Felix, Cammie, and a few other close friends were waiting. Robin came running in just then, eyes wide.

"What'd I miss?" Robin asked.

"It's a girl," she announced, not even bothering to fight the tears anymore. "A girl...named Valerie."

The others whooped and started hugging each other, talking excitedly until the doctor came by and ask them to keep it down for the sake of the sleeping babies and moms. She guided them to the hospital's newest addition—a celebratory bar, sponsored by Sandra and Diego and complete with wine and other drinks.

Not even the rain pounding on the windows could put a damper on the mood here, and when they went into the streets on a recommendation from Cammie, they all spun and danced in the rain until they were soaked, just laughing and enjoying this world they lived in.

It was a glorious occasion, and in the days that followed all of them took turns cooking and helping the new family in any way they could. But finally the time came for Cammie and Royland to return to Prince Edward Island, where they were going to settle down—though the others there had voted on a name change for the island, calling it "Queen Cammie Island," which she thought was stupid. Royland couldn't get enough of it.

They met at the docks, where Captain Reems waited to carry them north.

JUSTIN SLOAN & MICHAEL ANDERLE

"I'll miss you," Valerie said, hugging Cammie and then Royland.

"But you'll come up to visit?" Cammie asked.

Valerie glanced at them and then at Sandra and Diego, little Val sleeping in Diego's arms.

"I'd like that, but... Remember how Colonel Walton talked about space, and Michael? I don't know if it's just a feeling or what, but I sense the time is coming."

Sandra scrunched her nose. "You would leave?"

Valerie nodded with a cautious glance at her friends. "You all... I don't know what I will do without you, but you have your own lives now."

They nodded—all but Robin.

"I've been thinking," Robin said, eyes moving up to the skies too. "My parents are safe. I needed to be sure of that, and now I am. But I feel the call too. I have this power, and I want to use it to make a difference."

"You'd come with?" Valerie asked.

"If they'd let me," Robin replied with a shrug, "yes. I can't think of any better way to keep this world safe. If the war up there is anything like what we've been through, they'll need the two of us."

Valerie laughed and shook Robin's hand as if they were business partners, a playful smile spreading wide. "We'll bring 'em hell."

The rest agreed that any alien enemies out there had better watch their asses, then finished saying farewell to Cammie and Royland.

It happened as the five of them were on their way back to put baby Valerie down in her crib: a shadow fell over the city. At first they thought it was simply another storm, but then a familiar voice called out.

"Valerie, I hope this isn't a bad time," Michael said. They turned to see him walking toward them on one of the broad streets of New York. Behind him a silver shuttle hovered, and past that a space ship larger than anything Valerie had ever seen took up most of the sky to the east. It had to be several times as large as the whole city of New York!

"My... Dark Messiah," she greeted him, bowing her head. "Is it time?"

He smiled and nodded. "Terry-Henry Walton is already aboard and looks forward to seeing you again. He brought a friend, so I will extend the offer to you to do so as well." His eyes moved past her and he nodded. "Welcome, Robin."

Valerie had almost forgotten that he could read minds, so she blushed.

"Thank you."

"Say your farewells and let's be off. We have a war to win."

With that he turned and they watched as the shuttle dropped into the center of Capital Square. People had left a wide space and now watched in amazement. He moved forward and a door opened for him, and he stepped up into shuttle. They could just make him out as he sat there waiting. At first Valerie hadn't been sure it was him since his head wasn't completely bald like it had been when they had first met. As they approached, though, there was no doubt.

"So this is actually it," Sandra said, careful with the baby as she gave Valerie a one-armed hug. "Fuck! I mean," she covered the baby's ears and blushed, "I'm going to miss you, I really will. I'll write you, let you know how we're doing. If there's a way to get them to you?"

"I'll ask," Valerie promised. She hugged Diego too and then turned to the shuttle, her eyes moving to the large ship above with awe. "I have a feeling this is going to blow my mind."

"You and me both," Robin replied.

You two have no idea. Michael's voice said in their minds, and they looked at each other with wide eyes.

"Here we go," Valerie said.

"Into the great beyond to kick alien ass," Robin agreed.

"Let's make it count."

Together they gave Sandra, Diego, and baby Valerie a final wave, and walked forward to enter the shuttle and begin the next stage of their journey.

FINIS

AUTHOR NOTES - JUSTIN SLOAN

WRITTEN OCTOBER 1, 2017

The day a series comes to an end is a sad one, but not in our case. Why? Because it's not really the end of the series after all. Yes, the Reclaiming Honor series is complete at eight books, but you might have seen Facebook posts about Valerie going into space and figured that out from the end of this book. To be sure there is no doubt: we are continuing Valerie's story, but it will be in space.

She will continue to fight for justice and she will have a friend or two, and we'll have a fun little surprise for you all.

Surprises can be good!

But to focus on this book and what it took for me to get it here, let me tell you about the last couple of weeks as I was trying to finish it up. First, my grandmother is very sick with something that puts extra proteins on the brain in a related way to what Parkinson's does, and is probably going to pass soon. We just found this out about a month ago, and now her situation has deteriorated to the point where she can barely open her eyes sometimes, and can't ever leave the hospital room. So my wife and I decided I would have to take a couple days away from writing (aside from on the airplane) to go see her before she passed. I was very glad I did!

The time with my grandma reminded me how temporary our lives are, and how we really have to focus on what we love and who we love. Since going fulltime as an author, I have occasionally had moments where I wonder if I have to go back and get a job again. The money has been great, but I live in San Francisco and we're about to have our third kid. It's tough!

But after this, I'm more committed than ever to making it work. I love writing, and when I read your reviews and your emails I am incredibly inspired. I feel like I would be doing all of you and myself a great disservice to do anything but write full-time. Am I right? (Selfish plug time... you know, if you want to go write an awesome review, I'll certainly read it and cry for joy).

And then there are the moments where I'm tempted to take time away from my family to finish a book on time. We have to make our deadlines, right? Well, that's the other side of that trip —and the answer is NO! NEVER! We only live one life. That's the one life I get to spend with my amazing, encouraging wife. Only one life in which I get to have children, and only these days when they're still young enough to want to sit on my lap and just hug me without letting go. It's amazing. All of this is for them and so that I can have time with them, so how silly would I be if I gave up time with them so that I could meet a SELF-IMPOSED deadline? I love being reminded of this fact, because thinking about this gets me inspired and emotional. As much as Marines aren't supposed to be emotional (LOL!) I can't help it, and I love the feeling. I love feeling so inspired that my chest warms, my arms tingle, and my eyes start to tear up.

It's not a heart attack, right? Someone tell me if I'm confusing the two.

So, to get back on track... I went to visit my grandma, thinking that I could make up the writing time. No problem! I'm JUSTIN SLOAN, dammit! Of course I can do it.

SIGH. That was when I got really sick. I woke up the next day barely able to think, and for the next three or four days I was taking Nyquil like crazy and...wait, I'll spare you the details. The point is that life can get in the way, or death. We have to power on anyway, and you know what's crazy? Because of amazing editors like Lynne, and I mean AMAZING, we were able to pull it off!

Lots of hard work, motivation, and...still time with my family. This is the sound of me smiling. Get used to it.

And this is what it's like for me to finish a series. It's a gush of emotion, and I'm just so happy to be able to say that this isn't farewell, but a wave as we cross the street, only to meet back up farther up the road as we meet Valerie on her trip to space.

Guess what? It's not very far away, either!!! I'm excited to see where it takes us, to say the least. I hope you are too.

Thank you again for taking the time to read this series as well as my others, and for being such an amazing group of readers. We couldn't do it without you.

Justin

PS: One more thing... There's now a Facebook group for fan fiction in the Kurtherian Universe, if you want to join us there. It's starting to get off the ground. Maybe you can help us out with that! https://www.facebook.com/groups/TKGFansWrite/

Thank you, I cannot express my appreciation enough that not only did you pick up the eighth book, but you read it all the way to the end, and NOW, you're reading this as well. Since this book is part of a series, I am presuming you have blessed me by reading them all and what a fantastic feeling that is for any author!

So, we are at the end. Or, rather it's the beginning...or the end of the beginning but rather the new beginning after the ending.

You know what? Freaking Valerie is going to space...THAT'S what I'm trying to say, sheesh. I'm a writer, you would think I could get my freaking words on, but NOOOoooOOooo... I have to try and be cute.

Now, the Terry Henry Walton Chronicles (Craig Martelle) are done. Justin Sloan's Reclaiming Honor series is done and my own Second Dark Ages (The Dark Messiah) will be done by February – closing out the core series between the time of WWDE and The Age of Madness.

However, all of these characters live on. Two are going into the Age of Expansion and Michael and group will be going up into another area of space.

The Final Frontier, where no sane Vampire ever went chasing Kurtherians...Like...ever.

We have a LOT for you to enjoy and the series will EXPLODE here in November / December. Get your reading hats on and let's enjoy the fall.

The perfect weather to stay inside, light a fire, and read more books.

Thank you ALL for staying with Valerie through these books and as Buzz Lightyear would say...

"To INFINITY and BEYOND!"

Ad Aeternitatem,
Michael Anderle

BOOKS BY JUSTIN SLOAN

<u>SCIENCE FICTION</u>

RECLAIMING HONOR (Vampires and Werewolves - <u>Kurtherian
Gambit Universe</u>)

<u>Justice is Calling</u>

<u>Claimed by Honor</u>

<u>Judgment has Fallen</u>

<u>Angel of Reckoning</u>

<u>Born into Flames</u>

<u>Defending the Lost</u>

<u>Return of Victory</u>

Shadow Corps (Space Opera Fantasy - Seppukarian Universe)

<u>Shadow Corps</u>

<u>Shadow Worlds</u>

<u>Shadow Fleet</u>

War Wolves (Space Opera Fantasy - Seppukarian Universe)

<u>Bring the Thunder</u>

<u>Click Click Boom</u>

<u>Light Em Up</u>

Syndicate Wars (Space Marines and Time Travel - Seppukarian
Universe)

<u>First Strike</u>

The Resistance

Fault Line

False Dawn

Empire Rising

FANTASY

The Hidden Magic Chronicles (Epic Fantasy - Kurtherian Gambit Universe)

Shades of Light

Shades of Dark

Shades of Glory

Shades of Justice

FALLS OF REDEMPTION (Epic Fantasy Series)

Land of Gods

Retribution Calls

Tears of Devotion

MODERN NECROMANCY (Supernatural Thriller)

Death Marked

Death Bound

Death Crowned

CURSED NIGHT (Supernatural Thriller with Werewolves and Vampires)

Hounds of God

Hounds of Light

Hounds of Blood (2018)

ALLIE STROM (MG Urban Fantasy Trilogy)

Allie Strom and the Ring of Solomon

Allie Strom and the Sword of the Spirit

Allie Strom and the Tenth Worthy

BOOKS BY MICHAEL ANDERLE

For a complete list of books by Michael Anderle, please visit:

www.lmbpn.com/ma-books/

All LMBPN Audiobooks are Available at Audible.com and iTunes. For a complete list of audiobooks visit:

www.lmbpn.com/audible

CONNECT WITH THE AUTHORS

Justin Sloan Social

For a chance to see ALL of Justin's different Book Series
Check out his website below!

Website: http://JustinSloanAuthor.com

Email List: http://JustinSloanAuthor.com/Newsletter

Facebook Here:
https://www.facebook.com/JustinSloanAuthor

Michael Anderle Social

Website:
http://kurtherianbooks.com/

Email List:
http://kurtherianbooks.com/email-list/

Facebook Here:
https://www.facebook.com/TheKurtherianGambitBooks/